WHAT OTHERS ARE SAYING
ABOUT SKY ALEXANDER

The Fires of Love & Hate" is a sweeping historical saga!

—**Pam Brewer,** *The Idaho Statesman*

Great historical family drama

The Fires of Love and Hate is historical and family drama novel and it is the first in the series of novels about Hattie, an author's great-grandmother. The story of Hattie begins to take place in nineteenth century with her forced marriage and continues with how she deals with this tough situation.

The story is based on some real characters and actual events and that is what makes it even more interesting to read. Also, the book is well written, it is inspiring, easy to read and it really draws you into it.

I highly recommend it to any fan of family, romance or historical genre.

—**Yania, Amazon review**

An inspiring read with strong female characters

Sky Alexander's "The Fires of Love and Hate" tells the story of how a strong woman deals with an unwanted arranged marriage in nineteenth century America.

The novel, inspired by the author's family stories, is set in small-town Missouri, when the state's biggest wedding is about to take place.

I really enjoyed the characterization of the protagonist, strong-willed bride-to-be, Hattie Morran, whose poor father has offered her to be married to the cruel Abner Garland as payment for gambling debts.

Although Hattie is livid she is forced to marry someone she hates, she plans a way to gain the upper hand in the situation, which eventually results in her becoming extraordinarily wealthy.

"The Fires of Love and Hate" has a few underlying themes, the main ones being optimism, perseverance, and faith.

One of the strengths of the novel is the interesting dialogue, which is both engaging and realistic.

I feel the hands-down strongest feature of the novel is its cast of strong female characters. Regardless of the trials set in front of them, they remain determined and optimistic.

Overall, I found the book to be an inspiring, interesting read that is perfect for anyone interested in the historical-romance genre. I can't wait for the next book in the series!

—Rich Blaisdell

Great read!!

This book was great! Captivates you at the beginning and you find you can't put it down! You feel like you are right there with the characters. Loved it!

—Jo

The Fires of Love and Hate

This book is easy reading and becomes hard to put down as you get pulled into the lives of each character. You will find yourself rooting for Hattie and her family as they overcome the many trials life has in store for them. I loved the body guards! Especially Matthew! I can't wait to read the sequel!

—Theatre Girl

Best Historical Romance since Gone with the Wind!

Move over Danielle Steele and Elizabeth Cole… Sky Alexander is one of my new favorite Historical Romance authors. His writing is deep and emotional putting me right in the middle of the Western Romance that he has written. I bought this and read it nonstop…a real page turner. I love the fact that at the end of the book he lists all the release dates for upcoming books in the Fires of Love & Hate series. You really will love this Historical Romance and will mark it as one of the best that you have read in a long time. I can't wait for the next one.

—Scott Love

Awesome Book!!!

I absolutely loved, Forced to Love which is a historical romance. This book kept me wanting to read the whole way through and was just a book that i could not put down. Western romances like these are great and remind me how things might have been like in a historical romance setting. I would highly recommend Sky Alexander's Forced to Love it reminded me of Gone with the Wind.

—K Cowell

Classic Love Story!

Step aide Lily Graison, Carré White and Amber Adwell this new western romance made my heart sail and was absolutely one of the hands down best historical romance novels i have read in a long time. Sky Alexander's Forced to Love is sure to become one of the best western romance novels of the year.

—Kaikai Camilleri

HATE TO LOVE

Book 3 in The Fires of Love & Hate Series

SKY ALEXANDER

First eBook Edition: 2013
Second eBook Edition: 2014
ISBN: 978-0-9915836-4-5
First Paperback Edition 2013
ISBN: 978-0-9915836-5-2

The characters and events portrayed in this book are fictitious. Any similarity to a real person, living or dead, is coincidental and not intended by the author.

Falling into Love: a novel/by Sky Alexander

Cover design by © StoneHouse Ink

Published in the United States of America

"Our choices in life, define who we are and who we will become."
~ Sky Alexander

Chapter 1
CONSTANT CONFLICT

WITH NICK FAILING TO CONVINCE James that Hattie and Ira would be fine at their little farmhouse, Ira was becoming desperate. Thoughts of what Nick would do if he failed were flooding his mind, and it was driving him crazy. Before goodnights were extended, Ira sweetly took Hattie's hand and walked her out onto the front porch. "Darling, could you please talk to James yourself," he pleaded. "I really want to spend the week at the farm alone with you like we planned. After all, besides giving us a good scare, nothing really happened today."

Hardly believing what she was hearing, Hattie whispered angrily under her breath, "Nothing! You call someone trying to kill you, nothing? If I hadn't seen the sun reflecting off that rifle barrel and shoved you to the floor, I would have been a widow this morning even before I was a bride! We can't ignore what happened, Ira, and neither can my family."

"I'm not ignoring anything, and I don't mean for it to sound that way. It's just that I feel we can protect ourselves. After all, you do have twelve of the best gun hands in the country at your beck and call." Frustrated, his voice had risen considerably.

"Ira, for heaven's sake, keep your voice down. The last thing we need is a scene." Pacing back and forth, Hattie gazed out at the moonlit sky. "If we do go to the farm, where do you propose my men sleep, in that little barn? I'm afraid they'd be mighty uncomfortable, and I don't want to put them through that when I have this lovely mansion with living quarters for them right here on the estate. Those men protect me with their very lives. Why on earth would I want to make them miserable? I've never known you to be like this, Ira. Where's your compassion? Let's not forget, Dear, that it is your idea for us to go to the farm for our honeymoon, not mine. I wanted to go to Niagara Falls."

"But . . ."

"But nothing. I told you when we bought that farm that it would be all right to stay there during the warm months of the year, not in the dead of winter. We may be having an Indian summer tonight, but who knows what the rest of the week will be like. The weather changes awfully fast out here, you know. My men were hired to be near me twenty-four hours a day, and I will not have them suffer for my sake. If you insist on going out there or anywhere else, I expect provisions be made for my men ahead of time."

Hearing Hattie and Ira arguing, Minerva was saddened but not surprised. The day hadn't even passed yet, and there were Hattie and Ira, quarreling quite loudly right outside the parlor where anyone might hear them. Moving across the foyer to the front door, Minerva motioned to Matthew, who was just outside, to close the doors. Quickly doing as he was told, he stood listening in silence.

"Damn it, Hattie!" Ira argued, "Your men won't freeze to death. The barn's plenty warm enough for your men. We'll set up some cots, and they will be just fine. Don't over dramatize the situation. My God, you pay them a fortune to protect you; let them earn their money."

Amazed at Ira's lack of compassion, Hattie was totally disgusted. She had put up with some unreasonable demands where Ira was concerned in the past, but this was simply too much. Looking him straight in the eye, her voice was very serious. "You listen to me, Ira, and listen well. As far as I'm concerned, whatever I pay them isn't enough. They are the men that I have entrusted with my life, and I will not shortchange them."

"Well, that may be the way you see it, but I don't. As far as I'm concerned, we'll be safe. I'm sure I can take care of you, if you would just let me. Don't you have any faith in me?" He turned away and saw Matthew standing in front of the closed doors. With a hurt look on his face, Ira said, "Don't you think I'm right, Matt?"

Taking a deep breath, Matthew walked toward them. "Listen, you two, if you don't stop quarreling, someone inside is going to figure out what's going on out here, and you're going to have the devil to pay."

Knowing Matthew was right, Hattie closed her eyes and thought, "How could this be happening? Here we are on our wedding night, which is supposed to be the most wonderful night of our lives, and already, we're fighting." Always a peacemaker, she wondered, "What can I do to calm Ira down?" Tenderly she reached up and touched his shoulder, and even though it was against her better judgment, Hattie gave in. "Okay, okay, I'll do it, Ira. I'll talk to James myself. There must be something he can do to assure our safety and make the men more comfortable at the same time. I guess he could have them rotate in shifts of four around the clock. The last thing I want is to have my family sitting on pins and needles worrying about us the whole time we're gone."

Relieved beyond measure, Ira turned around with a smile, and pulling her to him, kissed her lovingly. "You're so wonderful, Hattie." Turning back to Matthew, he said, "When it comes to things like this, I remember all over again why I'm so crazy about her."

Standing on her tiptoes, Hattie waited for another kiss, but instead of kissing her, Ira lifted her into his arms and slowly turned around and around, finally setting her down and embracing her. Everything seemed perfect, as they stood motionless, bathed in the Missouri moonlight. Like porcelain figurines in a music box, they looked simple yet beautiful. Seeing them out on the porch and not knowing what had happened, Rebecca went immediately to the grand piano and proceeded to play a love song that Hattie had written.

Hearing the music, Matthew opened the doors allowing the melodic tune to drift out onto the front porch. The conversations in the parlor quickly died down as everyone went to the windows overlooking the porch to watch Hattie and Ira dancing in the moonlight. To the guests, they appeared in every way to be a happy couple dancing lovingly in each other's arms on their wedding night.

Wanting to include the whole family, Rebecca encouraged Dakota and Shannon to pick up their guitars and accompany her. Then, turning to the rest of the Morran family, she urged them to go to the doors and sing. Taking the lead, Laville's throaty contralto voice echoed harmoniously out into the stillness of the night. Hattie had purposely written it in her vocal range, and she sang it perfectly. Nick was astounded, not having heard Laville sing before. As for the guests, they stood mesmerized by the beautiful and perfect harmony of the Morrans' voices. One woman even remarked, "Is there no end to the unique talents of this family?" With Hattie and Ira in each other's arms waltzing in the moonlight, the scene that evening could not have been more beautiful or tender.

Standing in the shadows, Matthew and Minerva stood silent, hoping against hope that Hattie would be happy. With Ira so immature, they had their doubts, but only time would tell.

Later, after Hattie and Ira changed their clothes, Hattie went to James and her mother privately, pleading with them to find a way to assure her and Ira's safety at the farm. With grave concern, James reluctantly devised a plan. An hour later, she and Ira bid their leave and slipped down the back steps to their carriage, where Matthew, Cameron, and several men were waiting. Mounting their horses, they fell in alongside the carriage, as Ira carefully guided it down the road leading into the estate. The moon shone brightly as they rode, and the sounds from the mansion slowly drifted away. A few minutes later, the only sounds that could be heard were those from the horses' hooves. Hattie, trying to maintain a good mood, snuggled up against Ira's arm and asked as politely as possible, "Are you happy now?"

"Yes! After all we've been through, I thought this day would never come. I'm afraid if I pinch myself I'll wake up and find that it is all a dream."

As they reached the main road and continued riding in the direction of the farmhouse, the moonlight was streaming through the trees casting long eerie shadows on the ground, causing Cameron to wonder if Abner Garland was hiding among them. Just the thought of it made him cringe. Worried that he wasn't close enough to the carriage, he moved his horse in closer.

Seeing Cameron moving in closer, Ira felt uncomfortable. Even though he had gotten to know Hattie's bodyguards quite well in the past few months, he still didn't care for them being around all the time, and he especially disliked talking to her when they could hear him. So, speaking as quietly as he could, he leaned toward his new bride. "Hattie, I wish there was a way to make this last forever."

After thinking his statement over in her head, Hattie reached over, took the reins from his hand, and pulled the horses to an abrupt halt. With the moonlight so bright, Hattie could easily see the shocked expression on his face. "Ira, nothing lasts forever," she said calmly. "Life is too uncertain and things constantly change, no matter how much we want them to stay the same. Heck, not even our marriage will last forever. Didn't you hear Reverend Walker when he said that we were only married 'till death do us part'?"

"Well, yes, I guess." Hattie's boldness had caught him off guard. "I'm sorry, Hattie, it's just that everything seems so perfect," he replied, wondering when she had learned such wisdom, such deep thinking.

"Believe me, Ira, nothing is perfect, save the God that created us, but that notwithstanding, all that I care about is that you love me." Handing the reins back to Ira, she continued, "Now, I'm giving you the reins to these horses, just as I've handed you the reins to my heart. Don't ever try to mislead or mistreat me, and I promise I'll always be a loving and faithful wife."

Taking the reins, Ira sat dumbfounded. Her faith in him was so complete it took his breath away. Lowering his head, he despised what he was doing to her. His nerves were beginning to unravel, and his heart was breaking. He hated so much the charade that he was in and the lies that he was telling. "How, oh Lord," he thought to himself, "can I ever be forgiven for what I must do?" Snapping the reins, the horses began again, and Ira sat silent the rest of the ride. He wished he could do something, anything, but try as he might, he could not stop Nick's threats from consuming his mind.

After having spoken to Hattie earlier, James sent several men to the farm ahead of them. Since it was only a few miles from the mansion, it didn't take them long to check the place out, light a fire, and wait for Hattie and Ira. With kerosene lamps lit, the small farmhouse looked warm and cozy in the moonlight. Stopping out front, Ira lifted Hattie down from the buggy and held her in his arms, as Matthew made a quick pass around the house. Returning, he dismounted, and taking the reins to the buggy from Ira, he said quietly, "I'll take care of the buggy for you."

Still holding Hattie, Ira replied, "Thanks for everything, Matt. Hattie and I really appreciate it. Goodnight."

"Goodnight, Ira." Turning to Hattie, Matthew's voice was soft and understanding. "Try not to worry about anything, Hattie. If you need anything, we're only a heartbeat away."

"I won't, Matthew. Thank you." Just hearing his kind words eased her mind, and letting out a sigh of relief, she laid her head on Ira's shoulder.

Ira was pleased to see Hattie settling down, and he was thankful that Matthew had the uncanny ability to comfort her. From the very beginning, Ira had gotten along classically with Matthew, and he appreciated everything he had done for him. The other bodyguards, however, were a different story. Ira didn't much care for them, and it showed. Walking up the stairs with Hattie in his arms, he stood in front of the doorway and looked down at her. "Would you like to go inside or sit out here on the porch?" Just then, one of the Hattie's men opened the door from to the house from the inside and stepped out onto the porch.

"Evenin' Miss Hattie, Ira."

Ira, aggravated by his presence, chose his words carefully as to not appear angry. "Evening, Brigham, is everything all right?"

"Yes, Sir, everything's fine. James insisted Cameron have men posted several hundred feet in every direction from the house. I promise you and Miss Hattie that there won't be any problems while you're here." Nodding, he said 'goodnight', passed by them, walked down the steps, and disappeared into the dark.

With the door beginning to close slowly, Ira, still holding Hattie in his arms, kicked it open abruptly and stepped inside. Standing her to her feet, he turned and shut the door loudly, causing the windows to shake. The look on his face told the story, as he was visibly irritated, and looking into Hattie's eyes, he pleaded, "When is James ever going to let me run things?"

"Now, don't be like that, Ira," Hattie responded softly, trying to soothe him. "You know good and well you didn't have time to check out this place before we arrived. And don't you dare complain about the men. They are trying extra hard to be as unobtrusive as possible. Besides, you're the one who agreed to their presence here in shifts."

Still frustrated, it was becoming more difficult for Ira to control his feelings. "I just don't know who the hell James thinks he is, making decisions for us? We are perfectly capable of doing things on our own. Is this what I have to look forward to the rest of our lives?"

Trying to remain calm, Hattie was getting sick of Ira's pessimistic attitude. "James is concerned about me, Ira. He always has been, and after all the terrible things that have happened to me, I don't see a thing wrong with it."

Grabbing her hands, he pulled her near to him. "Hattie, I told you back at the mansion that I can take care of you. Now, either you believe me or you don't!"

Letting out a ragged breath, Hattie let go of his hands and paced the kitchen floor. She could hardly believe his constant bickering on their wedding night. "All right, Ira, if you really want the truth, personally I don't think you can. I think protecting me is too big a job for one man no matter how well prepared they think they are. Abner could be hiding anywhere at anytime, or just as easy, he could hire someone to kill me. That was no warning shot this morning, Dear. That bullet was meant for one of us. Now, if you want to get all bent out of shape over the fact that James loves me and watches over me, I'm afraid that's just too bad. You were the one who wanted to come out here in the first place and sent me pleading to James, who I might add, made provisions against his better judgment just so that we could enjoy our time here. He told me that the last thing he wants is for us to spend our honeymoon worrying and looking over our shoulders every minute." Shaking her head, she looked at him with bewilderment. "What's wrong with you, Ira? Good heavens, I thought you'd be grateful."

So overwrought about what Nick was forcing him to do, Ira didn't realize that he had overreacted. Now, he knew that of all things he shouldn't have done, he shouldn't have shown his strong dislike for James. Grabbing Hattie's hands again, he bowed his head apologetically. "Hattie, I'm sorry. You're right, I overreacted. Call it bridegroom jitters, I guess." Drawing her near, his voice got softer. "Do you forgive me?" Seeing her nod her head, he smiled brightly and kissed her forehead. "Great. Now, why don't you go outside and wait on the porch. I'll be right out with blankets so we can sit together and take advantage of the beautiful moonlight."

Watching him leave, Hattie stood shocked. She couldn't believe Ira's constant mood swings, but even more, she was tired of blaming herself for their disagreements. If this evening was an example of what their married life was going to be, it was obvious she had made the mistake of her life.

On the porch swing that night in the moonlight, Hattie snuggled in Ira's arms in an effort to drive the frustration out of her mind and wondered desperately what caused his violent mood swings. After many minutes with no answers her thoughts turned to God, and silently, she prayed, "Dear God, please bless us in our differences, and I promise I'll do everything in my power to make this marriage work for as long as we both shall live." Suddenly, that same foreboding feeling she often felt, gripped her heart with both of its icy hands. In her mind, she cried out frantically, "Dear God, what's wrong! Am I asking for too much?" Hoping for some sort of answer, Hattie was sorely disappointed, as all she felt was hopelessness.

Retiring for the night to the bedroom, Ira could not have been kinder or sweeter. He drowned Hattie in breathless kisses, and the sweet nothings he whispered with his sexy, baritone voice melted her like butter. Ira was no amateur at seducing women, and tonight, in his manly grasp with his gentle touch, Hattie didn't stand a chance. The hopelessness she had felt only minutes earlier was quickly replaced with a type of ecstasy that Hattie had only dreamed of. Lying still, she shivered as his fingers caressed her cares away. With the passion boiling inside her, she prayed that the night would never end, but when it did, she could not stop her mind from racing. Every touch, every kiss, and every word seemed permanently etched in her mind, and as she lay with Ira's arms about her, she thought, "Oh, God, if this is love, I hope it never ends."

* * *

AS HATTIE AND IRA's HONEYMOON week at the little farmhouse continued on, Hattie noticed that in the early evenings Ira often became restless and left for walks or went horseback riding alone. For the life of her, she didn't understand why he didn't ask her to go with him, but it was obvious that despite the wonderful first night that they had shared together, his mind seemed constantly preoccupied about something. At first she thought that perhaps Matthew and the other men were making him nervous, but he and Cameron had seen to it that her men were virtually invisible, so after a while she concluded that it must be something else. There had to be a reason, but try as she might, Hattie simply could not figure out what it could be. The one thing she did know, though, is that as the days progressed, her genuine feelings of love were quickly being replaced by feelings of despair. She could feel him pushing her away, even when they were in each other's arms, and to add to it all, she was beginning to feel sick for no apparent reason.

One morning near the end of the week, she woke up earlier than Ira, made coffee, and stood drinking a cup while she watched him sleep. He looked like a big overgrown kid, with his dark wavy hair lying across his forehead. Moving in closer, she observed a strange look of peace, which was set upon his face. Shaking her head, she knew it all too well. It seemed to only appear when he was sleeping. In silence, she thought, "Ira Saxon, I think my Mama was right. You're more than I bargained for. You're too complex, too moody, and too secretive. With all those things working against us, even your smile has a hard time lighting up my life." Finally reaching that conclusion, she wondered what it would take to reach that part of him he kept hidden so deep. Sighing, she said to herself, "I'll never give up, Ira, but if this marriage is to work, somehow I've got to find a way for us to be as one just like the good book says. We simply cannot spend the rest of our lives in 'constant conflict'." Finishing her coffee, she dressed and decided to take a walk while he slept. Stepping off the porch, she barely got five feet when Matthew stepped in behind her. He had been standing unseen in a nearby grove of trees, and as usual, he bore his patented Forsythe smile.

"Morning, Hattie."

"Good morning, Matthew."

"Going to walk far?"

"With the way I feel right now, walking to the end of the earth probably wouldn't be far enough." Turning around, she extended her hand, he took it, and for quite a distance, they walked together in silence. Looking up into his gorgeous face, she remembered again how thankful she was for him. "I'm so glad that James had you come to work for me last spring. I can't even begin to imagine my life without you in it." Suddenly and without warning, six men fell in around them. They had barely made a noise, yet Hattie felt their presence. "Morning, Gentlemen," she said with a smile, and in turn, they each replied cheerfully.

After walking for a way in silence, Matthew turned to Hattie with a concerned look. "Hattie, it seems to me that Ira's mind is mighty preoccupied with something. Does it seem that way to you?"

"Yes, absolutely!" she replied emphatically, thankful that someone else had noticed. Turning to the men, she asked, "Have you men noticed it, too?" In turn, they all replied in the affirmative.

Cameron, who was one of the six behind them, asked pointedly, "I've wondered, Miss Hattie, do you know why he keeps looking out the window and continually comes out on the porch? Are you expecting someone?"

"No, not a soul. We asked James to see to it that we weren't disturbed while we're here."

"Has he said why he goes out for a walks alone every morning, and why he rides off alone in the evenings?" Matthew asked, continuing the questioning.

"No, he hasn't. Do any of you know where it is he goes?"

"No, Ma'am," one of the other bodyguards replied. "He refuses to let any of us ride with him. He made that very plain the first day by telling us in no uncertain terms that he wasn't to be followed."

Stopping dead in her tracks, Hattie stood with her hands on her hips in defiance. "Well, you know what, Fellas, I don't give a hang what he says. Have someone follow him, Cameron, even if he gets irritated. I love him, but it's obvious that even after someone tried to kill us on our wedding day, he doesn't use good judgment." Turning to Matthew, she asked, "Tell me that most men aren't like that, Matthew."

"No, they're not, Hattie. Where most men are a little more cautious, Ira seems to throw caution to the wind."

"I feel something is terribly wrong, but no matter what I do, I cannot get Ira to open up to me. So, if following him is what it takes to find out, then so be it. Cameron, have your best man follow him, and if possible, try to make sure Ira doesn't see him. I want to know exactly what's going on. This secrecy of his has gone far enough."

"Ryan Teeples could do it, Miss Hattie. The man is less conspicuous than a Sioux scout."

"Fine. Have him follow Ira the next time he leaves."

"One more thing, Hattie," Matthew added. "I really worry about Ira's ability to protect himself. Most men feel they can take care of themselves, that's a given, but despite Ira's being a good-sized man and having adequate ability to defend himself with his fists, he's not worth a hoot with a gun. He needs to watch himself because a man wouldn't have to be too fast to take him."

Returning to the house before Ira awoke, Hattie cooked breakfast for them while he got ready for the day. During breakfast, Hattie was surprised by Ira's sudden interest in her business projects. Being as unobtrusive as possible, he asked many questions about upcoming ventures and highly confidential buy-outs and mergers. She thought it odd, but he assured her he was only interested for her sake. Thinking nothing of it, she gave him names and detailed information about many different company's upcoming transactions, forgetting completely her mother's warning about not telling Ira too much.

Her mother knew all too well that the worst thing you can do at the beginning of a relationship is divulge too much information. "Sometimes," Minerva would say, "you never tell them everything about you. It all depends on the level of trust and understanding that has been built between the two people involved. Love," she would emphasize, "is not always enough. If there is not enough trust and understanding in a relationship, there is no amount of love that can compensate." Then, for an example she would say, "For instance, I love Laville because she is my daughter and always will, but I would never tell her my most private thoughts or feelings, even if she was the last person on Earth. For as sure as the sun rises in the east, she would violate my trust by making light of my feelings, and she would use my secrets against me in a heartbeat, if she ever felt the need. Thus, it is imperative that you really know someone before you confide in them. If you don't, you are only setting yourself up for heartache and pain."

After they finished eating, Hattie continued the conversation by sharing her dreams of the future and talking about how they could help others with her fortune. But regardless of how hard she tried,

Hattie couldn't get Ira to talk about himself, his feelings, or their future together. It was almost as if he didn't even expect for there to be a future because every time she brought it up, he would say things like, "Geez, Dear, that is such a long way off," or, "A lot can happen between now and then." The feelings that she felt they should be having at this point, feelings of courage, hope, and confidence in the future, just weren't there. To make matters worse, she was feeling sicker with each passing day. "Something," she thought, "is completely zapping me of my strength."

The next day as Hattie and Ira were sitting in the porch swing wrapped in a blanket, Nick and Laville paid them a surprise visit. The weather had turned colder, just as Hattie thought it would, and now, even the days were frightfully chilly. Walking up to the house, Nick asked Hattie if he could talk to her about some property that she owned near his mill, which he was interested in buying. With Nick demanding all of her attention, Laville motioned for Ira to come talk to her by her buggy, which was the real purpose of their 'surprise' visit. As he walked in her direction, Laville spoke in whispers. "Hurry up, Saxon, for hell's sake we don't have all day."

Not liking Laville in the first place, Ira was irritated by her tone. "What in the world are you two doing here?"

"Why, checking up on you of course." Smiling smugly, she pulled her shawl further over her shoulder to protect herself from the cold breeze. Leaning to within in a foot of him, she questioned, "Are you giving her the poison?"

Dropping his head in shame, he replied softly, "Yes. Every night after she falls asleep I place three drops in her ear just like Nick said." Breathing deeply, he tried to contain his emotions. "You know how much I hate this don't you?"

Glaring at him, Laville responded curtly. "Ira, who the hell cares how you feel? Certainly not me, and I'm telling you right now if you don't come across, Nick will be the least of your worries. I have connections, Ira, and I'll have you and your family disposed of so fast it will make your head spin." Glaring at him, she made sure he knew she meant business. "Now, Nick wants you to go back to the mansion tonight. James and the family are getting restless having Hattie away from home, so Nick doesn't want to take any chances of them catching on to anything." Looking back toward the house, she saw Nick and Hattie approaching. "Shh! They're coming." Turning once more to Ira, she took her finger and ran it across her neck for emphasis. Sighing heavily, Ira knew exactly what it meant.

Approaching Ira, Hattie could see tension on his face. Getting into the buggy, Nick mentioned that they were on their way to the estate to talk to Minerva about their final wedding plans. Laville, meanwhile, sat silent and didn't say one word to her sister.

Looking toward Nick, Ira said somberly, "Tell Minerva we'll be home later this evening."

Watching the buggy roll away, Hattie grabbed Ira's hand. "Are you okay, Honey? You look tense."

"I'm fine, Hattie."

The way he said it left Hattie to wonder, but deciding to let it go, she asked, "When did you decide that we were going home this evening?"

"Well, it has gotten mighty cold in the last few days, and knowing how you feel about your men being in the cold, I decided it would be the best decision for all involved." He was lying through his teeth, but given the circumstances, he needed to score all the points he could with her.

"Really, Honey? That's wonderful." She was relieved beyond measure that he had finally come to his senses, but deep down, she thought the move was awfully suspicious, considering it was right on the heels of Nick and Laville's visit. Hand in hand, they walked toward the house in silence. Deciding to lighten the mood, she said, "I'm really glad you decided for us to go back to the mansion. The men will appreciate it very much, and heaven knows that I've got plenty of business to take care of with James before Lou returns."

Hearing James's name, Ira's said, "While we're on the subject of James, Hattie, I've been wondering, when would you like for me to take his place?"

Puzzled, she turned and looked at him. "What in the world are you talking about? Whatever made you think I would want you or anyone else to replace James? The man is brilliant. He's an attorney, he's my brother-in-law, and I trust him implicitly."

"I just assumed that once we were married, you would want me, your husband, to take control of things."

"Yes, you are my husband, Ira, but you are not Lou Alexander's husband. After all, Lou and I are partners, and any change in our organization would require our total agreement. I'm not putting you down, Dear, but to be able to do what James does would require your being an attorney, having his type of hands-on experience, and knowing all the right people. There will be plenty of things for you to do, but James will do what he does for as long as he sees fit. As I see it right now, there is no way on 'God's green earth' that Lou and I ever intend to replace him."

Dumbfounded, Ira realized now that Nick had been right all along. If anybody were to ever get to Hattie's fortune, James would have to be eliminated. As much as he hated to admit it, everything

Nick had said was falling into place. It was now obvious to Ira that James Kinnion had way too much influence, and no matter what, Nick would make him get rid of James too. Closing his eyes tightly, Ira wanted to scream. He hated being the pawn in this evil game of chess, but it was becoming ever more obvious that no matter what he did from this time forth, he was trapped with no visible way out.

Chapter 2
BOILING POINT

UPON HATTIE AND IRA'S RETURN to the mansion that evening, Hattie found her mother in an absolute stir over Laville's many costly, unreasonable demands for the wedding, and as usual, Dakota Jayne was doing all she could to calm Minerva's nerves. Seeing her daughter enter the parlor, Minerva called to her, completely exasperated. "This house, as large as it is, Hattie, can not begin to hold all the people on Laville's guest list. What on earth are we to do?" Letting out a ragged breath, she threw her hands up in the air and sat down on a nearby settee. Sitting down next to her, Hattie urged her to calm down. Looking at her close-up, Minerva knew instantly something was wrong. "Good heavens, Dear, what's wrong? You look pale."

"I don't know what's wrong, Mama. I feel weak and more sickly with every passing day." She was telling the truth, but trying not to dwell on herself, she said, "Anyway, I'm sure it's just a bug. Now, concerning Laville, please don't let her get to you. She knows exactly how unreasonable she is and how ridiculous her demands are. The only way to handle her is to beat her at own silly little game, by showing her how resourceful we can be. For instance, I can get carpenters out here and build temporary enclosures for the veranda. We'll get some wood stoves for heat out there like we did for Dakota's wedding in the court, and I'll have the inside walls and the ceiling covered in white, even if I have to buy every bolt of material in the state. That area alone will hold several hundred people comfortably, and we'll decorate it so beautiful, she'll be speechless."

Minerva looked in amazement at her daughter. Where most people would have been up in arms, Hattie didn't even bat an eye. Grabbing her hand, Minerva squeezed it gently. "All right, Honey, we'll do it, but I'm worried about you. You're extremely pale, and you sound tired. I'll send for Doc Cowley so he can check you over tomorrow or the next day. I just don't want to take any chances where your health is concerned."

"All right, Mama, I'd appreciate that. I really don't feel well."

"You know what else, Dear?"

"No, Mama, what?"

"You are absolutely amazing. You have such imagination and spunk. Where you got it, I'll never know."

"I got it from you, Mama. Don't you know that every good thing about me came from you? Your love and example has made me the person I am." Moving off the settee, she knelt at her mother's knee and kissed her hands. "You're everything any girl could ever want in a mother, Minerva Morran. And I really hope my daughter will be able to say the same of me one day. Being able to positively affect the lives of my children and help them to reach their full potential is my main hope in being a mother. If I can accomplish that, than I will feel that I have succeeded."

Clearing her throat, Dakota politely interrupted, "How was everything at the farm, Sis?"

Getting up and sitting again in the settee, Hattie fell back into her seat and sighed heavily. "Oh, Cody, it wasn't anything like I had hoped or thought it would be. Don't get me wrong, we had a wonderful wedding day and night, but the more I observe Ira's behavior, I'm afraid Mama was right, marrying Ira might have been a big mistake."

"Now, Hattie, It's only been a week. Give things time to settle down."

"I thought of that, Cody, and I discussed it at length with Matthew and Cameron. But something is really wrong, even they can sense it. Ira acts strange. He is distant, on edge, secretive, and moody, not at all like a man should be on his honeymoon. He spends most of our time asking questions and even asked me when I was going to put him in James's position!"

"You're kidding!"

"No, he was deadly serious about it. I can't believe how many times we quarreled, and about the most mundane things."

Listening quietly, Minerva feared that it would come to this. What she had dreaded all along was coming to be. Ira wasn't going to be a helpmate, as she had so desperately hoped. Instead, he was turning into a millstone wrapped tightly around Hattie's neck. And if allowed, he would drag her to the depths of the despair and unhappiness.

The remainder of the evening, Hattie spent with her little daughter, Katherine. During the honeymoon, Mary and Dakota had taken turns tending to her, but now that the honeymoon was over, Hattie was delighted to spend some quality time with her daughter again.

The next morning, she and James went right back to business. Working in her study, they immersed themselves in the work of trying to decide what was best for several companies, and after several hours, Hattie had to stop because she was having a terrible time concentrating on the work at hand. Leaning back in her chair, she was exhausted, mentally and physically. "James, I am tired of constantly being at odds with Ira and Laville. They are making me crazy, and I'm afraid if I don't maintain a good attitude toward them, everything I am doing for them will be in vain."

"Don't be so hard on yourself, Hattie. How anyone could manage to keep a good attitude with either of them for more than ten minutes amazes me. I, for one, have a really difficult time with Ira's moodiness, and Lord knows that no matter how much I try to show compassion toward Laville, she is a trial to my soul. What really amazes me, though, is how much you take from them, yet still love them and want to help them."

Smiling, Hattie appreciated James's kind loving words, even if they only calmed her nerves temporarily. Leaving the study, they joined Cody and Minerva in the parlor, just as the door slammed shut at the front of the house. Within moments, they heard the unmistakable sounds of Laville's heels, clicking on the marble floor of the grand foyer. Taking a seat beside her mother, Hattie prepared herself for the war of words that was about to follow, as meetings involving Laville were never simple or peaceful. A moment later, she stood in the open parlor doorway dressed in a gorgeous lavender dress that perfectly accented her voluptuous figure, and her raven hair was pulled up perfectly under an equally exquisite lavender hat. Standing in the doorway, her beauty was second to none. Tact, on the other hand, was an entirely different story. "So!" Laville bristled at Hattie. "You're *finally* home!" Walking further into the room, she turned to Minerva. "Mama, I thought of several more things I want added to my wedding list."

"Land's sake, Laville, except for inviting the Crown Heads of

Europe, I didn't think you could come up with anything else."

Letting out a laugh, Laville replied sarcastically, "Why, Mama, that's a great idea!"

Taking the list from her mother's hands, Hattie quickly scanned it. To her amazement, the list encompassed an unbelievable five pages. Looking up at her sister, Hattie's eyes were twice there normal size. "Just what is it you want added to this list, Laville?"

"Well, first of all, I don't care if it is Christmas, I don't want to see a speck of red. I want the whole house decorated in lavender and white."

"Your wedding will be right in the middle of the Christmas holidays, Laville. Even though lavender is a beautiful color, are you sure it would be appropriate?"

"Who cares if it's appropriate or not? Lavender is my signature color. I want lavender!"

"All right, all right," Hattie conceded. "I'll have the house decorated in various shades of lavender."

"Next, I want kerosene lamps lighting the road from the main gate to the house."

"Laville, that's over a half a mile of lights!"

"So? I want the lights!"

Taking a deep breath, Hattie muttered under her breath while she wrote on the list. "Lights, a half mile of lights."

"Both sides and down the middle."

Shaking her head, Hattie continued writing. "Lights on the drive from the road to the house, down both sides and the middle."

Hardly believing Laville's demands, Dakota interjected, "While you're at it, Laville, why don't you just summon God Himself to perform the ceremony?"

"Oh, how tacky, Cody. I don't remember anyone giving you any difficulty when you were married here."

"That's true, but I didn't demand the sun, moon, and the stars! I'll swear, Laville, it amazes me to think we came from the same planet, let alone the same family."

"You only make that remark because my ideas are more innovative than yours. Besides, Hattie can certainly afford whatever I ask."

"Well, that's typical of you," Dakota stated emphatically, "Always taking advantage of Hattie's generosity."

Trying to look hurt, she replied matter-of-factly, "Does it make me bad that I want the best in life?"

Turning red, Cody was boiling with anger. "No your outrageous demands make you bad! Good heavens, Laville, why can't you have a traditional wedding like everyone else?"

Tired of their arguing, Hattie decided to interject before things got out of hand. "Is there anything else you want on this list, Laville?"

"Yes, just one more thing. I'd like a European honeymoon."

Getting to her feet, Hattie handed the list back to Laville. "Here, finish this at home. I don't care what you want. I'll get it. I just don't want to hear any more fighting."

"You mean that?"

"Absolutely." With that statement, Hattie left the room. Then, popping her head back around the corner, she said, "Anything, that is, but the Crown Jewels." In amazement, she watched Laville mark through something on her list.

* * *

THAT NIGHT, HATTIE NOTICED IRA was unusually restless, hardly sleeping at all. Then, before daybreak, he left the house on horseback and didn't return until nearly noon. Glancing out a window, she watched him as he walked to the house, and seeing a look of deep concern on his face, she went to meet him at the front door. Opening the door and seeing her waiting for him, he faked a big smile, kissed her, and asked, "Miss me?"

"Yes. Where'd you go so early?"

"Riding."

"Did you see anyone or do anything special?"

"No, I just had to get out."

"Why didn't you wake me? I would have been glad to have gone with you."

"I didn't want to disturb you," he replied. The look on his face told Hattie he was lying, and he knew she could see it. "Look, Hattie, nothing happened. Trust me." The way he said it made chills run down her spine. Embracing her lightly, he retired to their bedroom.

Watching him walk up the stairs, Hattie knew exactly what she needed to do, and without a moment's hesitation, she grabbed a shawl from the hall closet and was out the door walking toward Silver Creek. She wanted to talk to Matthew, and knowing he would be the one to follow her, she kept walking waiting for him to catch up to her. Though cold, the day was calm and serene. Matthew caught up with her moments after she left the house, and reaching the Silver Creek, they chose a large fallen tree to sit on. After sitting in silence for what seemed like an eternity to Matthew, Hattie asked the question she had been dreading to ask. "Where did he go this morning, Matthew?"

"Ryan said Ira went to see Nick Starr. They met at the bridge just outside town, and their meeting ended in some kind of argument."

"Did Ira see Ryan following him?"

"No, Hattie, he didn't."

Rising to her feet, Hattie took Matthew's hand and urged him to stand as well. After he did, she stood silent, looking up at him, tears forming in her eyes. "I'm frightened, Matthew. Please stay near me. Something terrible is about to happen, I can feel it."

"I know. I can feel it too." Together, they walked along the Silver Creek and back to the house in silence. Stopping several times because she felt so weak, Hattie was having a hard time controlling her emotions.

Reaching the house, Matthew embraced Hattie tightly. Whispering in her ear, he said, "I'll always be here for you. You know that, don't you?"

"Yes, Matthew. That's one of the only things that I do know." Kissing him lightly on the cheek, she walked up the stairs onto the veranda.

"Remember," Matthew called out from behind her, "Doc Cowley will be out soon." Then, with his voice turning deathly serious, he said, "Make sure he checks you over, Hattie. You mean a great deal to me, and I hate to see you sick like this."

Turning briefly, she smiled at him. Then, continuing on, she walked through a side door and into the kitchen.

Seeing her sit down at the table, Mary stopped what she was doing and brought her a cup of coffee. "You sure be gettin' you a mighty strange one in Mr. Ira, Miss Hattie. He's not the same as he used to be."

"What do you mean, Mary?"

"Good-looker and a sweet-talker that one be, always tellin' a body what he be thinkin' they be wantin' to hear." Wiping her hands on her apron and pouring herself a cup of coffee, she continued, "But there be a strangeness about him now, Miss Hattie. Always bein' secretive, that one."

"You've noticed it too?"

"Yes, Ma'am. Everybody be a noticin'."

"Mary, let me tell you something. I'm absolutely worn out trying to understand what's going on inside his head. There are so many wonderful things I want to say when I'm alone with him, but I can't because I'm afraid to say anything for fear he'll misunderstand. I'm beginning to think there's something wrong with me."

"No, Lass, there ain't be nothin' wrong with you. You be tryin' your darndest where Mr. Ira's concerned, anybody here can be attestin' to that." Narrowing her eyes, Mary sat down next to Hattie, dropping her voice to whisper. "It be somethin' else."

Intrigued by her tone, Hattie's asked curiously, "What?"

"Well, you know I love you like me own daughter, and would rather cut off me own hand then be the bearer of bad news, but you best be watchin' your backside." Looking over her shoulder, Mary wanted to make sure they were alone. "I've been a seein' things with me own eyes. Mr. Ira may not be another Abner Garland, but he, Miss Laville, and Mr. Starr be up to somethin'. First off, Laville be a sneakin' to the farm to meet with Mr. Ira. Even before the honeymoon, they be a meetin' in secret back behind the barn. It not only be me a seein' 'em either, as the ranch hands have be seein' it also, and they be a tellin' me. Second, whenever Nick and Laville are here, they be a sneakin' off to all parts of the house to talk. They think secretly, but I be a seein' 'em, quarrelin' and meetin' in secret. One time, I even be seein' all three of them together. Mark me words, those three be in cahoots in some way, and I wouldn't be a trustin' a one of 'em. All this sneakin' around and private meetin' be a cause for wonder, and if ye be smart, you be listenin' to me warnin'. You be careful, keep your head square on your shoulders, and don't be blinded by love."

Startled by Mary's words, Hattie fell into deep thought. "Mary has to be right," Hattie thought. "I know her well enough to know that the last thing she would do is lie to me. But why would Ira be meeting with Laville? There certainly isn't any love lost between the two of them, that's for sure." Having the utmost trust in Mary, Hattie was anxiously looking for answers. "What could they be up to, Mary?"

"Don't rightly know, me darlin', but if it be me, I'd be a havin' Ira watched and followed? The fact that he be a meetin' with Miss Laville warrants your concern."

"I've done just that, Mary. Matthew has had Ryan Teeples following him."

"Good." Smiling, Mary could see Doc Cowley riding up to the mansion through the kitchen window. "It be lookin' like Doc Cowley is here, Lass."

"Thank heavens," Hattie said relieved. "I am so sick and tired of being sick and tired. I just have to get some answers."

"And what if he not be knowin' what the matter is?"

"Well, Mary, I tell you what, something's got to change. Because at the pace I'm going, I don't know how much longer I can last like this."

* * *

AS EVENING FELL OVER THE ESTATE, Hattie was still upset knowing that Ira had lied to her about not seeing anyone that morning, but wanting to evade another quarrel, she avoided saying anything during supper. She despised quarreling, and it had become far too prevalent between them. Ira, on the other hand, was his usual quiet self. Watching him eat, Hattie couldn't believe this was the same talkative, energetic boy she fell in love with only years earlier. He had always been doing something exciting growing up, and rarely was there a moment when he didn't have a smile on his face. But now, since Nick Starr had come into the picture, he acted like a beaten pup, edgy, quiet, and with a dark side that would unleash itself on you if you happened to strike the right nerve.

After leaving the dining room, he and Hattie began to walk toward the parlor in silence. Finally, after reaching the door to the parlor, she stopped, grabbed him by the arm, and turned him toward her. "All right, Ira, out with it! What in the world is wrong with you? You barely said two words at supper, and you didn't even eat most of your meal! I'm not blind, you know! You keep pushing me away, and I am getting plum sick of it! If we can't start to communicate, and I mean real soon, you won't have to worry about dying of old age because I'll shoot you myself!" Pulling out her revolvers that she always had in the slits of her dress, she aimed them at him. "Anything would be better than the silent treatment you're giving me, even jail."

Flying back in her face, Ira couldn't control his emotions any longer. Punching the wall behind her, he yelled at her at the top of his lungs. "Go ahead, Hattie, shoot me! I dare you! I don't care anymore! If it's not Nick trying to run my life, it's Laville! If it's not Laville, it's you!" Grabbing a picture on the wall, he threw it to the ground breaking it in two. Then, approaching her, he stared straight into her eyes with a look of anger so scary it chilled her soul. "You do what you have to do, Hattie, but as God as my witness, I've had enough." Turning, he stormed out of the house into the cold night and quickly mounted his horse. Because there was a full moon, he could be seen quite easily, and in tears, Hattie watched hopelessly through the parlor window as he rode off the estate, whipping his horse into a full gallop.

Moments later, Ryan Teeples followed on a second horse, while the family ran to the parlor where Hattie sat crying with her head buried in her hands. They had heard the yelling and came instantly. Minerva, James, and Matthew, seeing her raw emotions, urged the family to give them a minute alone with Hattie. Heeding their words, everyone left except for Dakota and Mary. Watching James close the doors to the parlor, they desperately wanted to know what happened, and with great concern for Hattie, they got as close as they could to the doors and listened in silence.

Following Minerva and Matthew to Hattie's side, James was angry beyond belief. Pacing the floor, he said aloud, "How many times, Ira Saxon, are you going to cause this poor girl suffering?"

Finally looking up, Hattie embraced her mother and laid her head on her shoulder, tears still streaming down her face. Bewildered, she asked, "Why does he push me away, Mama? No matter what I do, it seems to end up in a disaster."

"I honestly don't know, Dear, but I want you to know right now that it is not your fault. He has been acting strange for weeks. Like a pot of water, I guess he finally reached his 'boiling point'."

Hating to see her so distraught, James added, "I agree with Minerva one hundred percent, Hattie. Something's really wrong with Ira. He has completely closed himself off from us. I don't know what has soured him so, but you can bet that it has something to do with Nick and no doubt Laville. Mary just told us that she has been seeing them going around in secret. She said she told you earlier, but she wanted us to know as well. She says that a storm's a brewin', and she's not usually wrong."

Wiping the tears from her eyes, Hattie did the best she could to compose herself. Then, suddenly remembering Ira's words, she said, "That's it! While Ira was yelling, he said he had had enough of letting other people telling him what to do, mainly Nick. I didn't know they were at odds with each other, but it stands to reason, as he has been acting so strange lately." Taking a deep breath, she thought back to the look in Ira's eyes. Turning to James, Hattie was scared. "James, you should have seen the look in his eyes. It nearly stopped my heart. I've never seen a person so distraught in all my life. He is not in his right frame of mind right now, and I'm worried about what he might do."

Trying again to calm her nerves, James downplayed the situation. "Now, Hattie, let's not overreact here. He probably just went out to blow off some steam." Pausing, he took her hand. "Did he say anything else?"

"No, that's what was weird. He only said that he had had enough of Nick and Laville and me telling him what to do. Mary was right. He has been meeting with Laville, but it's not like she thought. The look in his eyes told the story, and the story is that he does not like Nick or Laville in the least. Something is terribly wrong, and it is because of them." Turning back to her mother, the tears began again to stream down her face. "I don't know what to do, Mama. For weeks, all I've prayed for was answers to what was wrong with Ira, but after what happened tonight, all I'm left with is more questions. And to make matters even worse, Doc Cowley had absolutely no answers as to why I feel so rotten." Looking skyward, she pleaded,

"Why, oh, God, is all this happening to me? All I ever wanted was to be happy, but all I've gotten is heartache and pain." Then, with her heartfelt words to the Almighty just barely fallen from her lips, a feeling of terror gripped her heart and chills again ran up and down her spine. Gazing out into the night, her instincts told her that after tonight, things would never be the same.

Chapter 3
SOMETHING'S HAPPENED

AS THE NIGHT WORE ON, everyone in the great house had retired for the night except for Minerva and Matthew, who were still sitting in the parlor with Hattie. The ticking of the grandfather clock and the fire dancing among the logs in the fireplace were the only sounds in the room. Feeling chilled, Hattie walked to the fire to warm herself. Standing quietly, she looked at clock on the mantle. "Five minutes till midnight," she thought, "and still no word from Ira." The past few hours of constant worrying had completely drained her of any energy, and her eyes were still puffy from crying so much. Turning, she listened to Matthew and her mother speaking about Nick and Laville. Walking toward where they were sitting, she said in a weary voice, "Aren't either of you tired?"

"A little, Dear," Minerva replied kindly, "but we decided we'd stay up with you until Ira has returned." Standing, Matthew walked to Hattie and placed his hand on her shoulder. "I think Mary was right when she said, 'A storm's a brewin'. So, with something so radically wrong with Ira and no real answers, we've decided to be your anchors in the storm."

"I can't tell you how much I appreciate that, Matthew. It means so much to know you all love me and that I have your support. You're right, though, something is very wrong. As Granddad used to say, 'I can feel it in my bones.' There was no logical reason for Ira's outburst before he left, and I am nearing my wits end when it comes to dealing with him. I've run his words over and over in my mind, but it still doesn't make sense. All I know is that his anger seems to be centered on Nick and Laville more so than on me, but because I am the one who sees him when he gets home, I get the brunt of his frustration. All that aside, however, I am deeply and truly worried. He left here so angry and determined, I'm afraid of what he is capable of doing while in that frame of mind." Pausing, she looked deep into Matthew's eyes. "I hope you know that I meant what I said to you earlier today, Matthew. I need you. This is one storm I definitely do not want to ride out alone." Her tone was soft yet firm, and Matthew knew she was deadly serious. Nodding his head, he waited for her to continue. "So, with that understood, why don't you and Mama go on to bed now? I'm about to turn in myself anyway, and I don't want to keep either of you up any longer." Agreeing, they said goodnight and left her alone in the parlor.

After blowing out some remaining candles on the night table, Hattie walked slowly to the stairs. Upon reaching them, she heard the back door open, and a moment later she was met by Ryan Teeples in the grand foyer. "Miss Hattie! Good, you're awake."

"What, Ryan? What is it?"

"Nothing I'm afraid," he said dropping his head. "It seemed for a while that Ira was headed for the mill, but on the way, he turned off at your little farm. He went inside while I waited and watched for him, but I never saw him come out. Finally, I decided to sneak up close to the house, and when I looked inside, the house was empty. So, not knowing where he went, I walked around back and found where another horse had been hitched for some time.

Evidently Ira had planned his escape from being followed."

Seeing his genuine disappointment, Hattie reassured him that it was okay. "Don't worry, Ryan, I'm sure you did your best."

"I believe he's been having someone watch to see if he was being followed." Once again dropping his head, he said, "I'm sorry."

As he turned to leave, she called him back. Hattie wasn't about to let him leave on such a sour note. She had big plans in mind for this young man. Calling to him, she waited for him to return to her. "Ryan, I'm curious. What is it you want to do with your life?"

"Well, what I really want is to be an attorney like your brother-in-law, James, but going back East to Law school costs a lot. That's why I'm so grateful I can work for you, Miss Hattie, because you pay me so well."

"But, Ryan, if you work for me for another year and a half, which is the length of your contract, won't that delay your education?"

"Yes, Ma'am."

"In that case, I'm sorry, Ryan, this arrangement just won't do. I'm afraid that after tonight, I'm going to have to let you go."

Shocked, Ryan's jaw dropped. "Did I do that bad, Miss Hattie? Listen, I'll go right back out and look for Ira again till I find him. The last thing in the world I want to do is disappoint you." Turning, he was ready to back out into the night to find Ira.

"No!" she said firmly. "That just won't do!"

Ryan was crushed. Grabbing her hand, he implored, "Miss Hattie, I need this job. I was really counting on going to school when my contract is up."

"No," she said shaking her head, "I'm sorry, but you don't need this job. I don't have any problem getting bodyguards." Looking down at him now on his knees, she smiled to herself and pulled him up. "What I do have is a genuine problem finding good, smart, and honest attorneys. So, if you'll accept, I'm going to send you back East to attend and complete law school, myself."

Regaining his composure, Ryan could hardly believe what she was saying. "But I can't go, not until I have enough money to pay for tuition, books, and living expenses."

Laughing to herself, Hattie led him over to a bench along the side wall of the foyer. "You don't seem to understand, Ryan; here's my proposal. I'll pay all your expenses, including living expenses, if you will sign a contract to come to work for me exclusively when you graduate. Is it a deal?"

"I . . . I . . . I don't know."

"I'll take that as a yes. Now, do me a favor while your tongue seems to be faltering. Please go upstairs and get a good night's sleep. James will go over all of the particulars with you soon enough, but right now, all I want you to know is that everything is taken care of." Pulling him close, she embraced him and proceeded up the stairs.

Watching her walk up the stairs, Ryan couldn't believe his good fortune, and thanked God for the blessing of Hattie in his life. It was a theme that would be repeated many times by many different people.

Retiring to her room, Hattie lay awake most of the night, falling asleep only occasionally. Then, when she did, she kept having the most horrible dreams. "Something is horribly wrong," she thought in desperation. "How could things have come to this? What could cause Ira to hold such anger?" Getting up more than once to lazily gaze out her window into the darkened sky, she couldn't get his words out of her head. "You do what you have to do, Hattie, but as God as my witness, I've had enough!" Watching the clock, the minutes turned into hours until finally, at a few minutes after three in the morning, Ira returned. Opening up the bedroom door as quietly as possible, he tried to slip in unnoticed. He hadn't fooled Hattie, though. She heard every move he made, and as he settled quietly in next to her, she wondered if it would be best to let him stew in his own juice or to confront him right then and there. Knowing full well what kind of argument they would get into if she did confront him, she decided on the former.

So, with neither saying a word, the remainder of the night was spent in silence, and as he lay deathly still next to her, Hattie couldn't shake the sudden foreboding feeling she was experiencing. "Something's happened," she thought to herself. "I can feel it." Praying silently for strength and guidance, she didn't know what was worse, the death-like silence of the night or the uncertainty and new questions that a new day would most assuredly bring. Falling asleep only occasionally, Hattie kept having a horrible recurring dream, in which she could see Laville standing with a gun in her hand and laughing diabolically. Then, raising the gun, Laville gave a smug smile and pulled the trigger causing Hattie to wake up covered in sweat. After the third time, Hattie sat up shaking with fear. "Laville," she thought silently between shudders, "you are amazing. Even in my dreams you seem to torment me." But as she lay back down, something inside told her it was a lot more than that.

* * *

IMMEDIATELY AFTER DAYBREAK THE NEXT MORNING, Sheriff Sanders and his deputies could be seen riding down the road to the mansion. George was the first to see them, but by the time he got over from the barn to meet them, they were already dismounting near the house. Walking quickly, the Sheriff went up to the front door, knocked, and was met by Mary.

Opening the door and seeing the Sheriff, Mary was visibly nervous. "Mornin' Sheriff."

"Mornin' yourself, Mary. My, you're looking good."

"Oh, that be a very nice thin' for you to say." Wiping her hands on her apron, she tried to appear calm. "What be a bringin' you to Silver Creek so early, Sheriff?"

"Well, actually, I'm here to speak to Ira, if I may?"

"Oh . . . really. Well, come right in and I'll be a fetchin' him for you." Taking him to the parlor, she saw that he was comfortable and went directly upstairs to Hattie and Ira's bedroom. Knocking softly, she called in to them.

Just waking up, Hattie looked at Ira as he answered, "What is it, Mary?"

"It's the Sheriff, Mr. Ira, he be a waitin' to speak with you."

Hattie, standing and walking to the big oval mirror, shook her head as she grabbed her hairbrush. "That's odd. What in the world would he want at this hour of the morning? Any idea why he's here, Dear?" Hattie made her question deliberately blunt, hoping to get some answers.

Staring straight ahead, Ira was unusually somber. "No." Then, walking over to his dresser, he slipped into some new clothes.

Amazed at his lack of concern, Hattie said pointedly, "Well, there must be some reason he's here. The Sheriff doesn't usually make house calls."

Looking directly at her, his eyes narrowed as he didn't appreciate her sarcasm, but instead of losing his cool as he often did, he kept his voice somber and calm. "I said I don't know, Hattie, but we'd better go find out." Turning, he finished getting ready.

Watching him comb his hair, she was at a loss. He acted and talked every bit like there was nothing to worry about, but yet, as she looked him over, there was something strange about his behavior, something unexplainable. "It's almost as if he already knows why the Sheriff is here," Hattie thought as she finished getting ready herself. Then, when they were both ready, they met Mary in the hallway.

Looking up at him, Mary looked at Ira with unusual look of worry. "The Sheriff be a waitin' in the parlor, Ira." Nodding, he let out a ragged breath.

Walking in between them down the hall, Hattie could almost feel the tension between them. There was no logical reason for it, but Hattie couldn't help but notice the stolen glances Mary kept giving Ira. Reaching the landing, Hattie said, "Mary, please dress Katherine when she wakes up and take her to Dakota."

Hearing Hattie's words, Mary's eyes got twice their normal size. Then, giving one last look to Ira, Mary replied quietly, "Sure thing, Lass, I be doin' it right now." Without another word, she was on her way, leaving Hattie flabbergasted.

Facing her husband, she knew something was going on. "What in the world is going on with Mary? Why did she keep looking at you like she was? Has something happened?"

Looking straight ahead, he didn't answer but instead proceeded down the stairs toward the parlor. Quickening her step, Hattie hurriedly tried to catch up with his long stride. As they reached the parlor door, she tried desperately to reason with him. "Ira, please give me some answers. Something is wrong, very wrong. I can feel it." Grabbing his arm, she turned him toward her. "Please, if you know what is going on, tell me now before we go in to see the Sheriff."

Hurrying to Katherine's room, Mary dressed her quickly, took her in her arms, and hurriedly went for Matthew then James. Within minutes, both men were up and dressed and met one another in the hallway.

Back in front of the parlor, Ira slowly looked down into Hattie's pleading eyes, and as he did, Hattie's knees grew weak as she saw, for the first time in her relationship with him, a new and unmistakable emotion: fear. She had never known him to be afraid of anything, yet the look in his eyes was unmistakable. Hardly believing it was Ira at whom she was looking, Hattie was violently shaken. Squeezing his arm, her voice was weak as she said, "My God, Ira, what happened?"

Hurrying to the parlor, Matthew and James stopped short of Ira and Hattie. It was obvious that something was very wrong.

Reaching out to Matthew, Ira took his hand. Speaking softly, Ira was having difficulty controlling his emotions. "Matt, do you remember what you told me back in Dakota, about being my friend?"

"I do."

"I'm going to depend on that now more than ever. Please, come in with us. I'm going to need you. The Sheriff is here."

"I know," Matthew replied.

Turning to James, Ira said quietly, "I'm going to need you too, James, but right now, I'd appreciate some privacy with Matthew and Hattie." Nodding, James understood.

Following Ira and Matthew into the parlor, Hattie was beside herself. Every second that passed made her more nervous, and try as she might to calm herself, she simply couldn't stop her mind from racing. "What on earth happened last night? Why is the Sheriff here?" Folding her hands, Hattie decided the only thing that she could do is pray and ask for help, and looking skyward, she said quietly, "God, please help us."

Seeing them enter, the Sheriff moved away from the fireplace and took his place in the middle of room, waited for everyone to take a seat, and finally turned to face them. Looking at them intently, he said,

"Hello, Miss Hattie, Ira, Matthew. How are all of you this mornin'?" His tone was friendly, but his face was void of all expression.

"We're fine, Sheriff. What brings you to Silver Creek so early this morning?" Matthew asked politely.

Looking carefully into the Sheriff's eyes, Hattie knew immediately that this was no social call. "Something is wrong, isn't it, Sheriff? Something happened last night, didn't it?"

Nodding his head, he paced the floor in front of them. "Yes, Miss Hattie, somethin' did happen last night." Looking directly at Ira, he asked pointedly, "Ira, mind if I ask where you were last evenin' around ten o' clock?"

Visibly nervous, Ira fidgeted in his seat. Breathing heavily, sweat began to form on his brow, as he thought desperately for what to say. Finally, after several seconds, he said, "Hattie and I were out riding."

Shocked, Hattie took her hand and smacked Ira clean across the back of the head. "Damn you, Ira! Don't you dare you lie to the Sheriff!" Glaring at him, her eyes were aflame. "I've taken quite a bit of crap from you, Ira Saxon, but I will not sit here and let you lie to a good man like Sheriff Sanders. Didn't anyone ever teach you that lying only gets you into more trouble?" Leaning back in her seat, she folded her arms angrily. "Now, tell him the truth."

As he sat rubbing his head where Hattie had hit him, Ira had a look of defeated anger on his face. He had hoped Hattie would cover for him, but as many people around town already knew, it was obvious that she didn't lie for anybody. Exhaling heavily, Ira spoke softly. "I went out riding by myself."

"Where did you go?" the Sheriff asked sternly. He did not appreciate being lied to.

Fidgeting in his seat again, Ira replied, "I went to blow off some steam."

"Blow off some steam?"

Irritated, Ira quipped, "Yes, blow off some steam. Hattie and I had a disagreement so I went out to blow off some steam."

"And where did you go to do this steam blowin', Ira."

Increasingly nervous, Ira looked to Matthew for help.

Seeing his look, Matthew interrupted, "First, do you mind telling us what this is all about, Sheriff?"

Pausing for a moment, the Sheriff looked Hattie over carefully, trying to see if she was wearing her revolvers under her dress. Unable to tell, he asked, "Miss Hattie, you aren't still packin' those special 45's are you?"

"Yes, Sheriff, I have them with me at all times. But, I'm afraid I don't understand what that has to do with anything?"

Shaking his head, he replied, "Well, I only mention it because I have the feelin' that thin's are going to get ugly around town." Stopping to take a breath, Sheriff Sanders could see they were hanging on his every word. Continuing, his voice was soft and carried genuine concern. "I guess there ain't no easy way to say this, so I might as well just say it."

Throwing her hands in the air, Hattie had reached her wits end. "For God's sake, Sheriff, what is it?"

Taking a deep breath, he turned and stared directly at Ira. "Nicholas Starr is dead."

Chapter 4
CONTINUAL SUSPICION

DESPITE THE FACT THAT HIS TONE had been very mellow, the Sheriff's words echoed through the parlor with the power and sting of a gunshot. Time seemed to stop, as the immensity of what had been said began to sink in. Sitting deathly silent, everyone was stunned. Even Ira, whose mouth had dropped completely open, shook his head blankly. Looking directly at him, Hattie's mind suspected the worst. After the way he left Silver Creek in such a rage the night before coupled with the fact that he lied about them riding left Hattie very suspicious. But to her surprise, his look wasn't the one of shame or regret or even sadness that she had expected. Instead, it was a look of complete and utter shock. Quietly pondering the situation, she thought, "Something about all this just doesn't make sense." Then, glancing at the Sheriff, she could tell by the look on his face that he was feeling the exact same way.

Curious for more information, Matthew was the first to say something. "Just exactly what happened, Sheriff?"

"Well, Mr. Forsythe, yesterday evenin', November 24th, at about ten o' clock in the evenin', Nicholas Starr was shot twice in the back just off the road to Gallatin in what looked like an attempted robbery. Though seriously wounded, he got away from his assailant and managed to get to old widower Sharpe's farm. Bill quickly went after

Doc Cowley, but despite the Doc's best efforts, Nick died just after midnight."

Still shaking his head in awe, Ira's mind was spinning like a roulette wheel with a million thoughts in it. Then, in an instant, it stopped, as he realized what this news meant for him. After all the pain and the anguish and the torment that Nick had caused him, he was finally and truly free. Closing his eyes, he let out a deep breath, and for the first time in months, a look of real peace fell over his face. In a single moment, it was if the whole weight of the world had been taken off his shoulders, and both Hattie and Matthew noticed it. Then, opening his eyes, Ira turned his attention to the Sheriff and in a somber voice said, "I'm sorry to hear that, Sheriff, Nick was a good friend."

Rolling her eyes, Hattie couldn't believe what she was hearing. "A good friend," she thought, "just yesterday he was fit to be tied with Nick, not to mention Laville. Ryan Teeples even saw them fighting, but now, after one mysterious night which included his death, Nick was a good friend again." Reaching over to grab Matthew's hand for support, Hattie's mind was racing. It was now clear to her why the Sheriff was there to speak with Ira, as he and Nick were known around town to be friends, but despite her best efforts to figure things out, Hattie was at a loss. "It was obvious," she reaffirmed to herself, "by his reaction that Nick's death was a surprise to him, but why lie about him being a good friend when they were clearly at odds? And why the sudden look of peace when this 'good' friend died?" Leaning back in her chair, Hattie was near her wits end. Nothing made sense, and she couldn't help but be unnerved by Ira's reactions. With her mind continuing to run in all directions, she finally settled on Laville. "Is Laville aware of any of this, Sheriff? She ought to know, being Nick's fiancé and all."

Sighing heavily, he replied, "Yes, she does. She was at Nick's side when he died."

"At midnight?"

"Yes, Miss Hattie, at midnight. What's strange is that no one knows who informed her of the attack on Starr or how she found him. She was just there."

"Well, why didn't she come here and tell us herself?"

Clearing his throat, he said softly, "I'm afraid she couldn't, Miss Hattie. She's under arrest."

"Under arrest? What on earth for?" Hattie voice's got continually louder, until she was practically yelling.

Raising his hands to calm her, Sheriff Sanders knew how touchy Miss Hattie was about her family, even Laville, so he chose his words carefully. "Look, Hattie, I had no other choice, but I promise you I will explain everythin' in due time. First, let's start with what we know for sure. Bill Sharpe told me that Nick reached his farm shortly after ten last night. Seein' how hurt he was, he immediately brought him into the kitchen and laid him on the floor on some sheets while he went to get Doc Cowley. Upon returnin', he was surprised to find Laville sittin' next to him holdin' a written statement as to what happened durin' his attack near the road. Considerin' they were engaged, he didn't think much of it at the time, and so, with Nick too weak to talk, Doc Cowley, Laville, and himself watched as Nick signed the statement with an X."

"What did it say, Sheriff?" Matthew asked, hanging on every word.

Looking Ira squarely in the face but without an accusing tone, he replied somberly, "The statement said that you attacked him, Ira, over money and the contents of his will. It said that you were jealous that he had named Laville his sole beneficiary, and when he wouldn't sign a new will that you had made up includin' you, a scuffle broke out."

"Why, that's a damned lie!" Ira exclaimed, not believing what he was hearing. "That's preposterous! Sheriff, think about it. Why would I want his money? I'm married to one of the richest women in the world for God's sakes. Don't you think that money is pretty much taken care of for me?"

"Yes, that's what I thought too, but we have a signed confession, Ira, witnessed by three people."

"Well, I'm telling you, I did nothing of the kind." Insulted, he began to rise up to leave but stopped when Hattie grabbed his arm and pulled him back down into his chair.

"Ira Saxon, don't you dare leave this room until we get to the bottom of this!" Looking him straight in the eyes, she was deadly serious. "Now, you just sit right back down here and start telling us the truth. You know darn well that you were at odds with Nick and that you have quarreled with him recently. I know that for a fact because I've had you followed. Ryan Teeples saw the two of you arguing on the bridge right outside town yesterday, and then, when you exploded at me last night, you told me that you had had enough of him controlling you. Now, I'm not a scientist, Ira, but I wasn't born yesterday, either. I know that you have lied to me about your relationship with Nick, and I also know that you didn't get along with him nearly as well as you'd like us to believe."

Listening quietly to Hattie's pointed words, Ira was very angry that she had been having him followed, but looking around the room at Matthew and the Sheriff, he knew that arguing with her now would do him absolutely no good. Grabbing her hand, he instead replied surprisingly calmly. "Hattie, you're right, lying does me no good at this point, but that's not what I was trying to do here. I know how this must look, but I didn't do those things. And the other night I wasn't arguing with Nick about money, I was arguing with him about . . ." Looking into Hattie's innocent green eyes, his voice trailed off.

"About what?" Hattie asked anxiously.

"Nothing," he replied quickly. Getting to his feet, he walked to the window of the parlor and gazed out over the barren fields of Silver Creek. Seeing the innocence in Hattie's eyes just moments before, Ira couldn't bring himself to tell her what he was really arguing with Nick about. "It would kill her if she knew the truth," he thought. Turning back toward the Sheriff, his tone was blunt. "Correct me if I'm wrong, Sheriff, but didn't you say that Nick's statement was signed only with an X?"

"Yes, Ira, it was. We questioned Sharpe and Doc Cowley both at length about that very thin', but they both stood by their testimony and maintained that he seemed coherent enough to know what he was doin'."

"Coherent? If what you said earlier was true, Nick couldn't even talk for Christ's sake! How, then, could he be coherent enough to sign anything, let alone convey to Laville all the rest of what happened near the road." Looking around at everyone in the room, Ira pleaded, "It just doesn't hold water!"

Standing in silence, the Sheriff had no response.

Seeing his arguing was getting him nowhere, Ira sighed heavily then asked, "So, just what else did this 'signed' confession state?"

"Well, this is where it gets rather graphic," he said softly, pausing momentarily. "The statement said that in the scuffle, you and Nick exchanged blows before he finally turned to run away from you, and when he did, you shot him twice in the back in cold blood." Stopping again, the Sheriff could see the shock of what was being said was more than Ira could bear, and falling into a chair, Ira stared blankly at the wall.

Continuing, the Sheriff turned his attention back to Hattie and Matthew, who, themselves, were having trouble accepting his words. "Now, accordin' to the statement, when Ira was reloadin' his weapon to finish the job, Nick crawled bleedin' and wounded into some dense trees for protection. Unable to find him, he gave up after several minutes, allowin' Nick to hobble the rest of the way to Bill Sharpe's farm a short distance away. But," he added emphatically, "that's not all. Bill Sharpe told me this in confidence this mornin' at the jail. He said that after everyone had left last night, he heard Laville talkin' with an unidentified man on the road by his house. He thought it was odd that she would still be out, considerin' all that had happened, and he decided to see what they were talkin' about. Approachin' them unnoticed, he was alarmed at what he heard."

"What?" Hattie asked anxiously.

"Well, you're probably not goin' to like this, Miss Hattie, but he heard Laville gloatin' to the man about what a good job Ira had done gettin' rid of Nick, and now that he was out of the picture, she could get her hands on his money. Given that information, we had to arrest her as an accessory to the murder. Sharpe said that it appeared to him that Laville and Ira were workin' together to get rid of Nick."

Finally regaining his wits, Ira's shock had now turned to rage. "That's not true!" Turning to Hattie, he knelt down in front of her. "It's not true, Hattie. You have to believe me. I've done a lot of crazy things in my life, but I didn't shoot Nick, I didn't want his money, and

I most certainly had not made a pact with Laville to get rid of him. For God's sake, I don't even like her." Getting to his feet, he gazed help-lessly at Matthew and the Sheriff. "You have to believe me."

Letting out a ragged breath, Hattie didn't know what to think. She knew that Ira had been meeting with Laville, and it didn't sur-prise her one bit to find out that she was involved, not after her fiasco with the Andersons. Deciding she needed more information, she asked, "Sheriff, have you actually seen this will that Ira had suppos-edly made up to name him as Nick's heir?"

"As a matter-of-fact, I have it right here," he said, handing it to her. "When Sharpe returned, Laville said that Nick had gotten it from Ira during the scuffle and then gave it to her as evidence."

Opening it up, Hattie recognized that it was Ira's handwriting. Calling him to her, she handed him the document.

Examining it, Ira's head dropped. "Yes, this looks like my hand-writing, all right, but I'm telling you that I never made out this will. It may be a secret to some, but I've been around this family long enough to know that Laville is a master forger. My guess is that she did this to frame me, and it appears she got her way, as there is noth-ing I can say to defend myself." Walking again to the window, Ira was beginning to feel defeated. His world was quickly caving in on him, and in his mind, there appeared to be no way out. Looking over his shoulder, he could see Hattie was crying. Walking quickly to her side, Ira tried in vain to wipe the tears away. He hated seeing her so distraught, and the last thing in the world she needed was more pain. Grabbing her hand, he spoke softly. "Listen, Hattie, I know how this must look, and believe me, the last thing I ever wanted to do is bring you pain. But, as God as my witness, I did not commit this crime."

Hattie, listening to Ira, said nothing, as tears continued to stream down her face. In silence she thought, "Ira Saxon, maybe you didn't kill Nick, but you sure do wrap yourself in 'continual suspicion'." Taking his hand, she pleaded, "How can this be happening?" More than anything, she wanted to believe him, but too many things were beginning to add up. Things that Mary and Ryan had seen, a signed statement from Nick himself, and then to top it off, a signed will in Ira's handwriting that substantiated Nick's statement. Fighting back the tears, she turned slowly to Sheriff Sanders. "So your reason for coming to Silver Creek this morning, Sheriff, is to arrest Ira for Nick's murder?"

"Yes, Ma'am, it is. I have no choice, and I hope, Ira, that you'll come peacefully. If you're as innocent as you say, then you shouldn't have any problem convincing the Judge."

Getting to her feet, Hattie felt sick, but as she walked to the doors of the parlor, she knew she needed to keep her wits about her. Opening the doors, she called to Mary. "We have a problem here, Mary, please call the family together. Ira and I have to go into town with the Sheriff, and I need to speak to everyone before we leave."

Within minutes, the entire family sat gathered in the parlor. James was talking quietly to the Sheriff, as Mary closed the doors behind her and took her seat next to George. Very concerned, she asked, "Miss Hattie, what this be about?"

Looking out into the faces of her family, Hattie hardly knew where to start. Her mind kept flashing from scene to scene, as she went over dozens of confrontations she and Laville had had during the past few months. Once again her mind stopped on the night Laville said that she had found Nick's will and had convinced him to name her as his sole beneficiary. Realizing she was stalling, she cleared her throat. "There is no easy way to say this," she said, pausing. "Nick has been murdered. The Sheriff is here to arrest Ira for the murder, and Laville is in jail as an accessory to the crime." Once again the weight of the words echoed throughout the room, and you could have heard a pin drop in the silence that followed.

Speaking first, Dakota said, "I'm sorry Hattie, but none of this makes a bit of sense to me. Why is Laville in jail and who said Ira killed Nick Starr?"

Turning to the Sheriff, Hattie asked him to please explain again to the family all that he had told Ira, Matthew, and her earlier. Upon his finishing, she turned to Dakota and asked, "Does that clear things up, Cody?"

"Not really," she said bewildered. "I don't even remember Ira leaving last night. I thought he was here at home with you, Hattie."

Amazed, Hattie replied, "Surely you jest, Cody. I thought everyone heard the argument that we had, didn't you?"

"No . . . I . . . guess I didn't."

Speaking up, Mary said nervously, "She hasn't been a feelin' well, Miss Hattie, and because of such, she just not be a rememberin' all the details of last night."

Heartsick beyond belief for her daughter, Minerva interrupted, "Is there any way out of this for us, Sheriff?"

"No, Minerva, I'm afraid not."

Turning to James, Hattie looked at him with desperation. "James, I know this is a lot to ask, but we're going to need you for Ira's defense. And Matthew, you and Lou, when she arrives back from Chicago next week, are going to have to take over part of James's workload. Ira is going to need a good attorney, as it looks as though the evidence is stacked against him. Everyone else, we need your complete support." Anxiously, Hattie waited for a response. "So, does everyone understand their roles?"

Nodding, everyone replied in a unanimous, "Yes."

Seeing everyone coming together on his behalf, Ira was having a hard time controlling his emotions. "What a paradox," he thought. "I have been nothing but trouble to this family, yet they are willing to come to my aid, and James, despite his personal feelings, is willing to defend my life in court."

Standing, Minerva approached the Sheriff. "Do you honestly think Ira shot Nick, Sheriff?"

"I'm not the Judge, Minerva, but with a signed statement from Nick before he died, the matter is deathly serious. There is no doubt that if Ira is convicted, he will be hung."

"Ira," Hattie pleaded, "you must cooperate with the Sheriff. He's only doing his job. You said that you're not guilty, so let's ride into town with him, and maybe we can get this mess straightened out today." Excusing herself, Hattie went upstairs to change and to put extra shells for her revolvers in her handbag. She didn't want to take any chances on safety, and the Sheriff was right. With Ira being brought in for Nick's death, things could get ugly.

Turning around to leave, she found Mary standing in her bedroom doorway. "What can I be a doin' to help, Miss Hattie?"

Sitting on the edge of her bed, Hattie invited Mary to sit with her. "Just stay here with me for a few minutes, please. I'm shaking like a leaf inside."

Breathing deeply, Mary took Hattie's hand. She wanted desperately to give Hattie hope, but she knew that the situation Ira found himself in was now beyond their control. Seeing that Hattie was near tears, Mary let go of her hand and embraced her. Patting the back of her head, she said, "Sometimes life be hard, me Lass. This be one of those times, and though we'd like to be able to be a doin' somethin', I be a feelin' that Ira's in the Lord's hands now."

"Oh, Mary," Hattie said between tears, "I hope Ira didn't kill Nick. I can't imagine who did, but somehow, I just know it wasn't him."

Kissing Hattie on the forehead, Mary helped her to finish getting ready. "Don't be a worryin' about little Katherine, Lass, she be fine with me."

"I love you so much, Mary. Thank you for all you do for her. Time seems to have flown by; I can hardly believe she's just three months away from being three years old."

As she and Mary reached the front porch, Hattie was disappointed to see that the Sheriff was about to place Ira in shackles. As several deputies and all of Hattie's bodyguards sat on horseback surrounding the Sheriff's buggy, the Sheriff said somberly, "Sorry, Ira, but I have to put these on you."

Touching the Sheriff's arm lightly, Hattie asked, "Does he really have to be shackled, Sheriff, with an entourage like I have?"

"Sorry, Miss Hattie, I don't have a choice in the matter."

After watching the Sheriff help Ira into the buggy and shackle him to it, Hattie took her place next to him. Laying her bible in her lap, she watched as the Sheriff took the reins. After riding a couple of miles, she asked quite abruptly. "Sheriff, can you unshackle Ira from the buggy and chain him to my wrist."

"That's highly irregular, Miss Hattie," Sheriff Sanders said with a concerned look. Then, looking into her eyes, he said, "but for you, I'll do it."

Driving into town several minutes later, she noticed small crowds here and there, and fearing for the safety of the group, the Sheriff, his deputies, and her men pulled closer to the buggy. "Are you expecting trouble, Sheriff?" Hattie asked worriedly.

"I'm not rightly sure, Miss Hattie. That's why I would rather you not be shackled to Ira."

"Well, perhaps you're right. I can shoot with my left hand free just as well as I can with my right, but given the crowds that are gathering, I think I'd rather have both hands free now." As Ira was released from her wrist, Hattie took out both revolvers and laid them on the seat on either side of her.

"I'm not expectin' any trouble until we reach the jail, Miss Hattie, and then I'm not quite sure what to expect. Nick was well liked in Gallatin, and unfortunately you, Ira, never have been. The fact that you've been accused as Nick's murderer is goin' to cause quite an uproar. Though it only happened last night, it's obvious word of it has spread pretty quickly this mornin'."

Sitting quietly, Ira knew that running with his cousins the Donovan brothers hadn't done his reputation one bit of good. They were known to be heavy drinkers, gamblers, and they often ran with loose women. So, what the Sheriff said about his not being well liked in Gallatin made perfect sense.

Approaching the Jail, they found a large crowd of angry people forming and a deputy trying to disburse them. Sheriff Sanders, who was old enough to be Ira's father, didn't relish the thought of stirring up a hornet's nest and said so. Hattie, hearing the Sheriff's complaint, decided she'd take charge herself. "After all," she thought, "the jail is only less than a hundred yards away.

Taking the reins from the Sheriff, Hattie stopped the buggy. Immediately, several men started toward them yelling obscenities, and before anyone realized what she was doing, Hattie took her revolvers in each hand and fired each of them several times in the air. "Okay," she said loud enough for everyone to hear, "you folks can just get the hell out of here before I forget I'm a lady and show you just how good a shot I am." Knowing exactly what a good shot she was and not sure what she might do, the crowd scattered faster than a bunch of chickens at mealtime, and as the buggy pulled up to the steps of the jail, Ira was taken quickly inside.

Once inside, Ira asked in a whisper, "It doesn't look good, does it Sheriff?"

"No, Son, it doesn't, and one thin's for sure, I'm not goin' to put you in a cell with a window. I'll need to board up the window in back on both sides, before I can put you back there. So for now, I'm going to trust you to stay right out here in the office with me, and I want your promise you're not goin' to try to make a break for it."

Looking down at his shackles, Ira gave him a weary smile. They both knew he wouldn't get far even if he wanted to run.

Before the Sheriff had a chance to fix the window, Judge Bowls, the traveling circuit judge came in and pulled him aside. "Better get some extra deputies, Sheriff," he said with deep concern. "Looks like things are getting pretty ugly outside. Who fired those shots?"

"It was me, Judge," answered Hattie.

Seeing Hattie, who had taken a chair in the corner, he smiled sympathetically. "I might have known it was you, Miss Hattie. Tell me, how are you faring through all this?"

"Right now, I don't know what to think." Looking around and failing to see Laville, she asked, "Sheriff, I thought you said that Laville was arrested too. Where is she?"

"She's bein' held in the Trenton jail, Miss Hattie. I almost wished

I hadn't had to arrest her. After Bill Sharpe's visit this mornin' at the jail, we stopped by her home in Gallatin before we made our way out to Silver Creek, and when we informed her she was under arrest, she was absolutely furious. Honestly, I think a wildcat would have been tamer than she was. She threw the biggest fit I've ever seen in all my born days, but even more astonishin' was the fact that she showed absolutely no sorrow or anguish about the death of her fiancé, Nick Starr. With the way she was carryin' on about Ira havin' killed Nick, I didn't dare put them in the same jail. So, I had her taken to Trenton."

Stepping inside and closing the door behind him, Matthew had a grave look of concern on his face. "Hattie, the crowd has regrouped, and now there are twice as many men and women outside as there were just a few minutes ago." As he was speaking, several shots were fired at the jail and rocks struck the door.

Hearing the shots, Hattie was furious, and before the Sheriff could stop her, she was outside on the porch. Standing as tall as her petite frame would allow, the wind played with her cape, picking it up and blowing it open exposing the beautiful white dress she was wearing. To make the scene even more dramatic, her hood, trimmed in white fur, blew off her head exposing her heavy auburn red hair, which danced nimbly around her shoulders.

With revolvers in both her hands, Hattie looked like an avenging angel. "All right you scalawags!" Hattie yelled at the top of her lungs. "Back off!" Pausing momentarily, she scanned the sea of faces before her. "You look like a lynching mob to me, and I don't like it. I'm giving you fair warning, right now, that I intend to shoot the very next one who fires at the jail. Standing where I am, I can shoot twelve of you in less than twelve seconds, and I don't care which of you I shoot!" Pausing again, she moved her revolvers back and forth across the crowd. "So, if you've got any sense at all, you'll get the hell out of here! Otherwise, believe me when I say you are in for a rude awakening!"

"You wouldn't dare shoot us, Miss Hattie, you ain't got no authority," a man yelled from the back of the crowd.

Hearing the man and knowing the predicament that Hattie was in, Judge Bowls grabbed the Sheriff and said, "Follow my lead, Sheriff, I think little Miss Hattie needs our help." Once outside, he stepped beside Hattie and yelled back at the man. "I'm afraid you're mistaken, Gilliland, because the Sheriff and I just deputized Miss Hattie less than five minutes ago." Standing silently, Sheriff Sanders couldn't believe the Judge was lying to the crowd, but seeing the looks on their faces, he chuckled to himself. Continuing, the Judge said, "She's madder than a bandy hen and you can just bet if she feels threatened, she's gonna shoot!"

Standing in amazement, Gilliland cried out, "Why in the hell would you deputize her, Judge? Have you gone completely crazy?"

"No rule about a deputy being a man, Gilliland, and Miss Hattie's more than qualified. She's the best shot in the state. You of all people ought to know that. If memory serves me, she pretty well cleaned up against you at last year's turkey shoot. Besides, who would protect a man better than his wife?" Nodding his head, Gilliland knew the Judge was right, and disgruntled, he walked away. "So, if there are no other concerns, I'd suggest that all of you get the hell out of here before I turn her loose."

"What makes you think Miss Hattie won't shoot the Sheriff and free Saxon, Judge?" Another man in the crowd yelled.

"Now, you all know Miss Hattie," the Judge said pointedly.

"Most of you have watched her grow up, and you all know that she's as honest as the day is long."

Defeated, the crowd slowly began to disperse, and as the Judge escorted Hattie back inside the jail, he said, "That's quite a temper you got, Little Lady. For a moment there, I thought you really intended to shoot somebody."

With a slight twinkle in her eye, she answered softly. "I guess we'll never know, will we Judge?" Letting out a weary laugh, she added, "Thanks a million for backing me up like that."

"My pleasure."

As he smiled brightly at her, Hattie felt, even if only for brief moment, that somehow things would work themselves out.

Chapter 5
HOPE FOR A MIRACLE

THE EVENING WIND HOWLED as the two men ducked into some trees off the main road for shelter. After walking several yards, they sat down on a fallen tree, and looking at each other, they wondered how long it had been since they'd last seen each other. The man with the dark overcoat spoke first, as he warmed his hands with his breathe. "Abner," he said through shivering teeth, "why in the hell have you called me out here tonight? It's freezing."

Looking at him with narrow eyes, Abner opened up his satchel exposing countless gold pieces.

The man's eyes grew large as he slowly surveyed the sparkling treasure. Running his hands through it, his interest was peaked. "Okay, you have my attention, Abner, but you still haven't explained why you telegrammed me, forcing me to come out here into the wilderness." Leaning forward, he wanted some answers. "Come on, what is this about?"

"All this could be yours," Abner said pointedly. "All we ask is that you cooperate."

Looking around for another person, the man asked, "We?"

"The person whose money this is of course."

"And who would that be?"

Laughing, Abner tossed the satchel into the man's lap. "Stanley,

Stanley, Stanley, you always did ask too many questions."

Staring him straight in the eyes, Stanley Johnson replied, "I'm an attorney, Abner, that's my job."

"Yes, it is. That is your job, and that is what we're counting on, you doing your job." Leaning toward him, Abner abruptly grabbed Stanley's coat and yanked him toward him. Reaching into his pocket, Abner pulled out a gun. "You better understand right now that we mean business, Stanley." Waving the gun in front of him, Abner pushed him back down on the fallen tree.

Considering how far back they went, especially having been the best man at his wedding, Stanley was shocked and insulted that Abner had resorted to using a gun on him. Fixing his coat, he spoke softly but distinctly. "You know, Abner, I would have thought you would have been grateful for all I've done for you."

"Grateful!" Abner cried out angrily. "You think I should be grateful to you? You in your big house in Gallatin with all your prestige and power, thinking you have the world by the tail. Hell, you wouldn't even be there if Pa and I hadn't helped you." Glaring at Stanley, Abner's blood was boiling. "I've spent the last two and a half years trying to forget what my stupid mother and that bitch Hattie did to me, but even after all that time, the wound is still sore. Yet, you want me to be grateful. Ha, what a joke!"

Stanley's shock now turned to anger. "Damn you, Abner! You have no right to come down here and threaten me, much less belittle me for what I've achieved. Yes, you and your Pa helped me, but as I remember, that was part of our agreement. And the other part of our agreement that you so conveniently fail to recall is that I would help you if you ever happened to get into any trouble. Well, Abner, not only did you 'happen' to get into trouble, but you have seemingly

made it your life's work." Standing up, he paced back in forth while
he talked. "I don't know how many times I've thrown false leads to
the Sheriff just to cover your ass. You're a smart man, Abner, no
one denies that, but with as many horrible things as you've done,
you would have surely been caught by now if it wasn't for the help
that I have given you." Pausing, he looked directly into his eyes.
"That, my friend, is the sad truth."

Standing to face him, Abner pointed the gun right at his
head, but then, as the sting of Stanley's words was replaced by the
realization that he was right, he slowly lowered the revolver. Clearing
his throat, his voice was somber. "Here's the deal, Stanley. No more
fooling around. Ira Saxon killed Nicholas Starr last night right outside Sharpe's farm near Gallatin. You need to get on the case and
go after him. My silent partner and I want him hung for it, not life
in prison or anything else. He has to die." Glaring at Stanley, Abner's
words echoed into the night. "The gold in the satchel is only one-
third of what you'll get if you can accomplish this for us. Furthermore, my partner will remain silent until such time that they deem it
necessary that you meet. But I'm warning you, Stanley, if you try to
go behind our backs, I'll hunt you down. Understand?"

Nodding, Stanley understood perfectly.

"Good. Then you know what to do." Placing his gun back in
his holster, Abner hurried back to the main road and within seconds
was off on his horse, leaving Stanley to ponder their meeting.

"Good old Abner," he chuckled to himself, "always up to no
good." Then, shaking his head, he ran his hands through the gold
pieces again. Most people would have been intimidated by Abner's
threats, but Stanley, knowing him as well as he did, knew that Abner
couldn't afford to get rid of him, especially now. So, with the satchel

of gold in his hand, Stanley's thoughts were smug. "Ira Saxon, I hardly know you, but with all this gold in front of me, I don't care." Breathing in the cold night air, he couldn't help but smile. "With any luck," he thought silently, "After this trial is over, I will be a very rich man."

* * *

REACHING THE STEPS OF DOC COWLEY'S OFFICE, Matthew knocked lightly on the door. As he waited for an answer, he pulled his coat tighter to shield himself from the bighting cold. After several seconds, the door opened and Matthew hurried inside. "Hello Doc," Matthew said politely as he hung up his coat and kicked off the fresh snow that had just begun to fall in the night.

Leading him into his office, Doc Cowley had a concerned look on his face. "Thank you for coming, Matt. Before we begin, tell me, how is Hattie holding up tonight?"

"Truthfully, I know it's killing her inside having to see Ira in jail, but outwardly, she is handling the situation with as much grace as possible." Taking a seat in a chair by the fireplace, he continued, "She refused to leave Ira's side at the jailhouse and actually had us set up a cot for her in his cell." Shaking his head, he warmed his hands by the fire. "The amount of her compassion and size of her heart never cease to amaze me. I left Cameron with her and headed right over as soon as I heard you wanted to talk." Sighing heavily, he leaned back in his chair. "So, what did you want to talk about?"

"The examination I did on her the other day," he replied earnestly.

"What about it?"

"Well, when I first looked at her, I didn't know what to think. She had no visible signs of anything being wrong, yet all the symptoms she described reminded me of a poison that I had heard of several years ago at a conference in Chicago. A doctor that I was meeting with there described it as the perfect poison, as it was totally undetectable. According to him, the mobs of Chicago and New York were using the poison to eliminate those who opposed them. Given in a large enough dose in a drink, in food, or on a gag rag, it is deadly, but alternately, if it is given in small doses over time it will slowly break down the person's immune system until they are so weakened, any virus can kill them."

"And you think that this is what was happening to Hattie? That she was being poisoned?"

"Well, Matt, like I said, I wasn't sure, but the symptoms of this poison are exactly the same as the ones that Hattie described to me. Loss of Appetite, extreme weakness, and blood in the stool are a few." Pausing, Doc Cowley sat in the chair next to Matthew. "Now, where things get really interesting is when I examined Nick right before he died, I found a vial of an unknown substance in his shirt pocket. At the time, I didn't think much of it because I was trying to save his life. But once he died, I took the vial and came back to my lab to look at it, and as near as I can tell, it is the poison I just got done telling you about."

"Really," Matthew replied in amazement. "So, you're telling me that you think Hattie was being poisoned."

"Yes, and somehow, Nick was part of it because this poison is not your everyday rat poison. It is extremely rare and hard to come by. Him having it on him when he died tells me that he was involved, probably with Ira, in poisoning Hattie."

"Ira? You think that Ira was the one poisoning her?"

Shrugging his shoulders, he said, "You said yourself the day I came out to check on Hattie that Ira seemed to be up to no good, as he was acting very edgy and secretive. Couple that with the fact that Nick and Ira were widely considered good friends and I think you have the answer to Hattie's sickness. My only guess is that they were after her money."

"Amazing!" Matthew exclaimed as he got to his feet. Walking back and forth in front of the fire, he scratched his chin while he thought. "Do you suppose that could have been what caused Ira to kill Nick?"

"It could have been. I honestly don't know."

"Well, think about it. What if Ira finally came to his senses and tried to stop what he was doing to Hattie. I'm sure that would have made Nick very angry, and if a scuffle had followed like the statement Nick signed said, Ira's only option would have been to kill Nick, not only to get him off his back but also to cover up his involvement in poisoning his wife." Pausing, he looked the doctor square in the eyes. "He would have had no other choice."

* * *

THE HOURS PASSED BY SLOWLY for Hattie that first night at the jail. She kept thinking that the whole sordid mess was somehow her fault, and even though nothing could have been further from the truth, she harbored guilty feelings. Then, as she awoke to a new day, Hattie decided that the time for pity was over. As her Granddad Elijah used to say, "Self pity is the height of unrighteousness and only dooms you to continued misery." Continuing on, he would explain, "If you truly want to make a change in your life for the better, you, and no one else but you, need to take the first step." Then, in conclusion, he would say with a big smile, "Remember, Heavenly Father will help you, but he only helps those who help themselves after all they can do. Faith without works is dead."

Reflecting on her Granddad's wise words, Hattie knew what she had to do. "This was not my fault," she told herself forcefully. "But I still have the responsibility to defend my husband and carry myself with dignity." So, with that as her goal, Hattie decided that she wasn't going to let Ira go down without a fight. He had been arrested on a Friday, and early Monday morning she met with James at Silver Creek to discuss their strategy. Sitting at her large mahogany desk in her study, Hattie was very determined. "This whole thing doesn't make much sense, James." Looking skyward, she continued, "I just can't see Ira killing Nick for his money. He could have come and gotten whatever amount he wanted from me, and then, the fact that Nick signed his confession with an X bothers me deeply. If he was in such a stable state of mind, why didn't he sign his full name?" Looking back at James, she said pointedly, "Those two things are what we need to concentrate on."

"I agree with you one hundred percent, Hattie. There are too many holes, but unfortunately, I think we are going to have an uphill battle. The Sheriff informed me yesterday after church that Stanley Johnson will be prosecuting this case, and he's seeking the death penalty."

"Really?" Hattie replied, as the wind literally seeped out of her sails. Leaning back in her chair, Hattie knew, just as James did, that Stanley was one of the best attorneys in the state. He hated losing, and he would stop at nothing to accomplish his goal. Standing up, Hattie walked over to James. Taking his hand, she said, "Even with him as the attorney, I feel we have a strong case. All we need to do now is show the twelve jurors the same holes that we see."

"And then?" James asked wearily.

"Then," Hattie shrugged, "we hope for a miracle."

Chapter 6
GUILTY AS SIN

AS JAMES WORKED FEVERISHLY to put together a solid defense for Ira, the days began to flow like a river, and before Hattie knew it, over a month had vanished. Secretly, she had hoped throughout December that Ira would somehow be allowed to return home, but with the dawn of a new year come and gone, she knew it was simply not to be. Looking back, Hattie recalled the events of the past month in a letter she wrote to Rebecca, who had to make an unexpected business trip to New York City.

Dearest Mother Rebecca,

It is hard to believe that it has been six whole weeks since Ira's arrest. I can't seem to get him off my mind of late, and every time I see him holed up in that tiny jail cell of his, my heart nearly breaks. I know he isn't perfect, Mother Rebecca, but I can't help but feel for him and his family. Andrew is taking things especially hard, and I honestly don't know how he would handle a guilty verdict. Stanley Johnson is showing absolutely no mercy in his quest for conviction, and after the way he has stirred up the whole county against Ira, I seriously doubt that James can find twelve honest jurors who haven't already made up their mind as to his guiltiness.

Well, I suppose I better catch you up on all that has happened since my last letter to you in which I told you about Ira being incarcerated. The Coroner held an inquest on Nick Starr's death the week after Ira's arrest. The verdict of the Coroner's jury, which was impaneled at the inquest, stated that Nicholas Starr came to his death by two gunshots to the back with Ira as the primary suspect. The preliminary hearing requested Ira be held to await action of the Grand Jury.

During the days that followed, there were rumors of a lynching party, and on a Tuesday night, Ira was taken from the Gallatin jail to the Kingston jail in Caldwell County for safekeeping. But after there was no trouble for several days, Sheriff Sanders returned Ira to the Davies's County jail at Gallatin, where he was to remain until the hearing, which is scheduled for January 15th, 1899.

I still can't believe that they had to move him like that, but that's only one of the amazing events that unfolded in December. Laville, who because she was having unmitigated fits nearly every day over at the Trenton jail, forced the Sheriff there to beg Judge Stepp to somehow expedite her case. He, like us sometimes, Mother, wanted her desperately out of his hair. So, on December 19th, the judge scheduled a special term of Circuit Court to hear her case. As court convened that day, it was obvious that Laville's case was far more lenient than Ira's, even though she was originally charged as an accessory in the murder. The prosecution had very little evidence to back up their case, and what evidence they did have was only hearsay. Bill Sharpe testified against her, but

it was her word against his, and after a short time of deliberation, the court had no other alternative than to dismiss
the case because of lack of evidence. Laville walked away
scott-free, wealthier than she's ever dreamed, and was home
for the holidays. Amazing, huh? I honestly don't know how
she does it.

To tell the truth, Mother, I still haven't figured out Laville's involvement in this whole mess. I know she was definitely talking with Ira before Nick's death, and unlike most
of the people in town, I believe that Bill Sharpe heard her
saying things the night of the murder. Unfortunately, I can't
prove any of it, but like Mama always says, 'Where there's
smoke, there's fire.' And I can't in good conscience believe
that Laville had nothing to do with it.

Anyway, I was so glad to hear in your last letter that you
will be home next month. It has been tough to get through
all this without you here, as you had just barely gotten home
for the wedding when you had to leave again. If it wasn't
for Lou getting back from Chicago so speedily, I really don't
think I would've been able to handle things. She and
Matthew have been my rocks in this storm of life. So, until
I see you in February, I wish you nothing but the best on
your travels.

Love,
Hattie

* * *

WHEN THE DAY OF THE HEARING arrived and Ira was
brought before the Judge, James immediately issued a plea of not

guilty. Still, an indictment was found against him for murder in the first degree, with a penalty of death by hanging. Court was adjourned and the trial was set to begin on Wednesday, February 25th, and the next two days were consumed in selecting a jury from sixty men, of which very few appeared to be honorable to James and Hattie. It was almost as if the county gathered together the worst candidates possible. Thus, James had very little to work with.

After the selections were made and the twelve men sat in the box, Hattie couldn't help but be disgruntled. "These twelve," she asked James sarcastically, "are going to decide the fate of my husband?" Seeing him nod wearily in the affirmative, she shook her head and said, "Lord, help us."

In the weeks before the trial, James worked even harder to scrape together every last bit of evidence and testimony possible. When the day of the trial finally arrived, James was walking through the halls of the courthouse to the courtroom when he ran into Stanley Johnson.

Sporting his usual smug smile, Stanley pulled James aside and said, "Kinnion, I hate to burst your bubble, but Ira doesn't have a snowball's chance in hell. We've got a signed confession witnessed by three people, we've got motive, and you and I both know that Ira had plenty of opportunity. With all that against him, this could be the shortest trial Missouri has ever seen."

Angered deeply by Stanley's callousness, James replied coldly, "Didn't they ever teach you in law school that men are innocent until proven guilty? Besides, even with all your 'evidence', there are holes in your case. Everything you have is circumstantial at best."

"Oh, for hell's sake, Kinnion, own up to the facts. Ira is guilty, and you know it." Looking at James closely, Stanley said with a slight smile, "You aren't seriously entertaining his cockamamie story about being framed, are you?"

"Maybe not," James said solemnly, "but I do believe in justice. And Ira deserves a fair and honest trial, even if he is guilty."

Rolling his eyes, Stanley turned to walk away but was stopped as James grabbed the arm of his suit coat.

Looking at him intently, James's tone was very serious. "You see, Stanley, it's people like you who corrupt this world. You, with your quick judgments, hardened heart, and lack of compassion, are a disgrace to the human race, and verily I say unto you, you will have your reward." Pausing, he pointed skyward. "If not in this life, then in the next."

As everyone filed into the courtroom, the tension was thick and the mood was dark. Standing, Stanley took his place behind the prosecution's desk on the right, while James settled in behind the defense's desk with Ira on the left. In the row of seats behind James and Ira sat Matthew, Hattie, Dakota, Minerva, Lou, Ira's family, and finally Rebecca, who had just days earlier returned from New York. Andrew was visibly worn out from the last three months, and his health, according to Emily, was getting worse by the day. Shannon, Robert, and John stood in the back of the courtroom by the Sheriff, while Laville, instead of sitting with the family, sat directly behind Stanley along with Doc Cowley and Bill Sharpe, the two other principal witnesses for the prosecution. Hattie thought it was quite rude of Laville to separate herself like that, but, "Then again," she thought, "it is Laville. She doesn't care about anyone's feelings but her own."

Hattie's bodyguards were spaced evenly throughout the courtroom, and the rest of the numerous seats were taken up by anxious townspeople. The death of Nick Starr had been the hot topic around Davies County ever since it happened, and now that the day of the trial had finally arrived, every seat was filled. Looking around, Hattie could feel the cold stares and hear the careless whispers. There was no doubt why the people were there. They wanted to see justice served, and as Hattie glanced back at Ira, she knew their idea of justice wouldn't be satisfied until Ira had hung.

The State's case commenced at eight o'clock on a Wednesday morning with the honorable Judge Stepp presiding. After the opening statements, Stanley began introducing his principal evidence. First, he showed the court the ante mortem statement of Nicholas Starr himself. "This statement," he said soberly, "is ironclad truth of the events that unfolded that fateful Night of November 24th."

Introduction of the ante mortem statement was strongly objected to by James, who argued that if Nick's mind wasn't clear enough at the time the statement was taken that he couldn't as much as sign his own name except with an X, it shouldn't be accepted. Unfortunately, after Stanley brought Bill Sharpe and Doc Cowley to the stand to testify that Nick was of sound mind when he signed the statement, James's objection was overruled.

The second piece of evidence Stanley submitted was a copy of the will that Ira had allegedly created for Nick as part of Ira's motive for murder. Stanley maintained that it was a part of a larger agenda that Ira had for getting a hold of Nick's vast holdings.

Once again, James objected vehemently. Speaking plainly, he said, "Your honor, why in the world would my client be interested in money when he is married to one of the richest women in the world?"

"Because some people can never get enough," Stanley replied

quickly. "Your honor, I'd like to call the County Clerk, Gus Dawson, to the stand."

As Gus approached the stand, Ira hung his head.

Sitting back down, James noticed Ira's reaction and asked, "What's wrong?"

"I don't have a good feeling about this," Ira stated somberly. "I feel that my past sins are going to come back to haunt me."

After Gus had been sworn in with an oath to tell the truth, the whole truth, and nothing but the truth, Stanley approached him and asked, "Have you ever spoken to that man?"

Seeing him point to Ira, Gus responded, "Yes."

"And what was the topic of your conversation on the day of November 1st?"

"Ira needed a marriage license," Gus replied calmly.

"But that was not all that was talked about, was it Mr. Dawson?"

"No."

"Would you mind telling the court what else was said in that conversation?"

"Sure." As Gus cleared his throat, everyone sat forward in their chairs. "I talked with Ira at length about many things that day, but the part that stuck out in my mind was when I asked him how it felt to be marrying a woman as rich as Miss Hattie."

"Why did that part stick out in your mind, Mr. Dawson?"

"Well, it was his response. It was quite surprising, actually."

"And what was his response?"

Staring straight ahead, Gus's voice was soft, yet distinct. "Ira answered rather hatefully that he had little need of Miss Hattie's money, as Nicholas Starr had far more money than anyone was aware of and that he knew exactly how to get it."

As Gus's words rang through the domed courtroom, the audience gasped in amazement. Even James, who had tried desperately not to form any opinions as to Ira's guilt and who did not know of Ira's encounter with Gus, could see their defense crumbling before them.

Hearing Gus's statement, Hattie's heart nearly broke. Glancing at Andrew, she could see tears beginning to form in his eyes, as Emily, Mary, and Hunter tried in vain to console him. Turning back toward the front, Hattie watched in anger as Stanley strutted back to his seat like a proud peacock. "How dare he act so callous," she thought. Then, to Hattie's amazement, as he was sitting down, she saw Laville give him a wink. Unable to believe what she saw, Hattie glared at Laville.

Seeing Hattie's angry look, Laville simply turned away.

"Oh, damn you, Laville," Hattie thought, frustrated, "Why is it that I feel you are the one who is 'as guilty as sin'."

As the trial moved on, Stanley brought up several other witnesses who reaffirmed Gus's testimony. They each stated in one way or another that they had heard Ira making comments about Nick's fortune, leaving little doubt in the jury's eyes that Ira wanted to get his hands on Nick's wealth. Watching them step up to the stand one by one, Ira could only shake his head.

Then, to throw fuel on an already raging fire, Stanley called Laville to the stand to seal the deal. After she took her oath, he had her corroborate the earlier testimony of Bill Sharpe and Doc Cowley concerning the ante mortem statement, and at Stanley's insistence, she further went into detail about the circumstances surrounding how she found Nick, all the way up to his death. Throughout her questioning, she played on the crowd's sympathy for the loss of her fiancé. Using her patented theatrics and crocodile tears, she had not only the jury but also the townspeople eating out of the palm of her hand. It didn't matter whether she was telling the truth or not, for with as well as she played the victim, most everyone in the courtroom believed her story beyond a shadow of a doubt.

Finally, just before she was excused, Laville turned to the jury and said, "I must say that even with the knowledge of Ira's troubled past, I couldn't believe that he could do something so horrible, but I guess it's like they say, 'sometimes the people you think you know the best, you really know don't know at all'."

"Very true," Stanley responded in agreement, "very true indeed." With that, Laville was excused, and given her very damaging testimony, it appeared as if Ira's fate was sealed.

Looking to wrap things up, Stanley's last order of business was to convince the court that Ira had the opportunity and time to commit the murder. "He has no alibi," Stanley stated coldly to the jury. "Even his family didn't know where he was during the time of the murder." Pausing, he walked right up to the jury box. "Sad as it is, friends, this is simply a case of a man getting caught with his hand in the cookie jar. You have a signed confession by the deceased pointing out his assailant, undisputable evidence and testimony of motive, and finally, it has been proven that there was ample time and opportunity for the accused to commit the crime." Taking a deep breath, Stanley paused for a moment. Then, turning to the audience, he said in a booming voice, "Ladies and gentlemen, the evidence is clear. Ira Saxon is guilty."

Almost immediately, thunderous applause arose from the townspeople in the crowd. One man even yelled, "String him up!" Needless to say, they were convinced.

As Judge Stepp tried in vain to calm the crowd with his gavel, Hattie, who was in utter shock over what was happening, decided to take things into her own hands. Standing on her chair, she drew her revolvers and yelled, "Enough!" Waving her guns back and forth over the crowd, her eyes were aflame. With silence falling over the crowd immediately, Hattie continued. "All of you disgust me," she said emphatically. "Only a coward rejoices in another man's misfortune." Pausing, she looked at them one by one to make sure her point got across, and then, getting down off her chair, she turned to the Judge and said, "Sorry, Your Honor, you may continue."

Nodding appreciatively, he turned his attention to the townspeople. Taking a deep breath, the Judge was having a hard time stifling his anger. "I do not tolerate outbursts in my courtroom," he said plainly. "So, if I hear one more word out of any of you, you will be thrown out of the courtroom immediately. Have I made myself clear?"

"Yes," the townspeople said in unison.

"Good. The floor is yours, James."

"Could I have a short recess to talk with my client, Your Honor?"

Considering all that had just happened, the Judge quickly agreed, and with a bang of the gavel, the court stood in recess.

Turning to Ira, James sighed heavily. "I was hoping I wouldn't have to do this, Ira, but I'm going to have to call you to the stand."

"Absolutely not," Ira answered without hesitation.

"Look, Ira, I don't like this any more than you do, but Stanley simply has too much evidence on you. Granted, some of those witnesses looked like they were lying, but their testimonies, along with Gus's and Laville's, if true, are very damaging. The only way that we can even hope to salvage our case is to have you give your account of what happened the night of the murder. Given that you maintain you are innocent, there shouldn't be a problem."

Shaking his head, Ira spoke softly. "Well, you're right about one thing, James. Those witnesses were lying because I never had conversations with any of those men except for Gus. But it wasn't at all like he described. Hattie's fortune didn't even come up. Instead, he was very interested in Laville's impending marriage to Nick. After he asked me what I thought about it, I told him that it was a shame that Nick and Laville were getting married because it only put her money-grubbing hands closer to his fortune, which was larger than anyone thought."

"Really?"

"Yes. I didn't even give it much thought until I saw him taking the stand today. Then I remembered our conversation, among other things."

"What other things?"

"Well, several years back while I was running with the Donovan brothers, we played a prank on Mr. Dawson while we were drunk, and he was mad at us for a very long time."

"What did you do?"

"We left the gate to his stable open one night, and his prized horse, which he loved very much, ran off. To this day, I don't know how he found out that we did it, but he did. When I saw him that day for the marriage license, I apologized to him, and I honestly thought we had buried the hatchet. Unfortunately, it appears that was not the case because he lied about our conversation."

Seeing the discouragement on Ira's face, James leaned toward him and patted his shoulder. "That is why you need to take the stand, Ira. You need to get up there and set these things straight."

"I can't take the stand, James," Ira said frustrated.

"Why in the world not?"

"I just can't okay."

"Can't or won't."

"Won't."

"Ira, this is your life we're talking about. You don't have any other choice. If you don't get up there and tell your story, the jury has no choice but to believe the testimony of those other people, even if they are lying. For God's sake, Ira, why won't you take the stand and take a chance at salvaging your life and clearing your name?" Looking into Ira's eyes, James could see tears forming, and immediately, he knew something was very wrong. Grabbing Ira's hand, James spoke with grave concern. "Please tell me what's wrong, Ira. I can't help you unless you confide in me."

Dropping his head slightly, Ira swallowed hard. Wiping tears away from his eyes, he spoke softly. "If I take the stand and tell the truth," Ira stated earnestly, as he looked up into James's face, "I will ruin even more people's lives. And I can't do that. I could never live with myself."

"What do mean? Whose lives?" James asked bewildered.

Sitting quietly, Ira said nothing. Looking over his shoulder, he could see Hattie and Dakota talking to his father, trying their best to keep his spirits up. "How could it have come to this," he thought, his mind in a daze. "All I've ever wanted to do was make my father proud." Taking a deep breath, Ira closed his eyes for a second. Opening them slowly, he turned again to face the front of the courtroom. "James," he said solemnly, "I've went about life very wrong. I thought that money and power would make me happy and more respected, but all it has brought me is heartache and pain. You see, in my quest for the vain things in life, I've hurt many people, and the weight of my sins is almost more than I can bear." Pausing, Ira took a deep breath. Then, dropping his head into his hands, he said, "So, James, even though I may not have committed this crime, I am not going to cause anyone any more pain." Raising his head up, he stared him right in the eyes. "That is why I can not and will not take the stand."

Awestruck, James knew there was nothing else that he could say. Ira had made up his mind, and nothing was going to change it. Sitting back in his chair, James stared ahead blankly until the Judge reappeared. Standing, he walked slowly toward the jury. With his whole plan thrown out the window, he was visibly nervous, and though he felt that Ira was innocent, he couldn't understand why Ira seemed to be protecting someone. "Who," he thought desperately, "would be worth going to the gallows for?"

So, after calling members of Hattie's family along with Hattie herself to the stand to serve as character witnesses with little result, as Stanley tore them apart in cross-examination, James had nothing else to do but pour out his heart and soul to the jury in his closing argument. He pressed over and over again the fact that it didn't stand to reason that Ira would be interested in money belonging to Nicholas Starr, when Hattie, his wife, was an extremely wealthy woman. That, coupled with the fact that Nick's ante mortem statement was signed with an X instead of his actual signature, left too many unanswered questions to convict a man of murder. "Ladies and gentlemen of the jury," James pleaded, "despite all the evidence laid out here today, there is still a reasonable doubt that Ira did not commit this murder. And according to the law, if there is any amount of reasonable doubt on a case with such far-reaching implications such as the death penalty, you must acquit the person."

Taking his seat, James held slight hope that he had made an appeal to the juror's hearts, but as he looked back, he could tell by their faces that they had already made up their mind. Devastated, James felt that the whole trial had been well planned and well executed by someone who could pay off witnesses and have Ira accused and convicted. "Something," James thought, "about this trial is rotten, and I, for one, intend to find out what really happened."

The only person who James and the family thought was completely fair throughout the trial was Judge Stepp, and both Ira's and Hattie's families felt like Ira was lying to protect somebody. As Hattie told her mother when Ira wouldn't take the stand, "He's protecting someone, Mama, I just know it. No one in their right mind would miss a chance to defend themselves unless they were trying to cover something up."

The case was finally given to the jury about five o'clock in the afternoon. Taken to their room by a sworn officer of the court, the jurors were left with strict instructions that if they arrived at a verdict, they were to remain together until the next morning, when everyone would once again be present for the verdict.

Hattie, Matthew, Andrew, and Emily spent a few hours with Ira at the jail, doing all they could to keep each other's spirits high. Finally, as it was getting late, Hattie and Emily left the jail for a walk with Matthew following silently behind. It was cold, clear night, and with new snowfall crunching under their feet, they made their way to Judge Stepp's home. Before heading over to the jail, the judge's wife, Barbara, had invited them for a late supper, and they decided to take her up on it, as they were starving. As they walked along holding hands, they realized that they had become more like sisters than sisters-in-law.

Emily had been holding tightly to the thought that Ira was innocent, but after the day's events in the courtroom, she said humbly, "As much as I'd like to believe otherwise, I see no hope for Ira, Hattie."

Agreeing, Hattie replied sadly, "Neither do I, Emily. I think what James told us after the trial today was absolutely right. Someone did a perfect job in planning all of this, and I'm afraid they've succeeded."

"I'll tell you what I believe," Emily responded emphatically. "Nick wasn't shot over a few paltry dollars. I'm not sure about my brother's innocence anymore, but I believe that Laville had just as much, if not more, to do with Nick's murder as Ira did." Walking slowly, Emily shook her head in disgust. "Sitting over there by herself all smug, she had guilt written all over her. And then that performance on the stand, why you would have thought she was auditioning for a Broadway show." Pausing, she looked up at up Hattie with deep anger in her eyes. "Don't you agree?"

"Unfortunately, yes I do," Hattie said softly, as they approached the gate to the Judge's home. "I've tried really hard to find a reason to believe in her innocence, Emily, but her testimony today was the last straw. It may not have been obvious to most, but I've dealt with Laville long enough to know when she's lying. And though she swore to tell the truth, the whole truth, and nothing but the truth, I'm afraid all we got were lies, more lies, and nothing but lies. In fact, I'm surprised that when she put her hand on the Bible it just didn't disintegrate. Laville's never told the truth in her entire life . . . why would she start today?"

Chapter 7
THOUGH YOUR SINS BE AS SCARLET

AT NINE O'CLOCK SHARP the next morning, the jury filed one by one into the courtroom. As everyone got to their feet, Ira was asked to turn and face them. The foreman of the jury, Harry R. Shipley, took his place in front and anxiously looked out over the crowd. Breathing deeply, he was amazed at the number of people who had turned out for the verdict. He thought there had been a large audience yesterday, but now, with people standing everywhere around the edges of the courtroom, he assumed the size of the gallery had doubled. Given the number of people present, there was no mistaking that the entire town wanted to know the outcome of Ira's trial.

Clearing his throat, Harry's voice trembled as he began. "Gallatin . . . Missouri, Feb. 26, 1899. We, the jury, find the defendant, Ira Drue Saxon, guilty of murder in the first degree as charged in the indictment."

As Mr. Shipley's words tumbled down like an avalanche on the people in the courtroom, Ira stared straight ahead emotionless. Ira's sisters immediately started crying, and Ira's father, Andrew, could only hang his head. Still in shock, Hattie didn't move, and though she was heartbroken inside, she kept her chin up and tried to appear calm. She had been preparing herself for weeks for the possibility of a guilty verdict, but now that she was actually in the courtroom hearing the jury's decision, the finality of everything made her weak. Grabbing Lou's hand for support, Hattie couldn't believe it was over.

The verdict itself was unprecedented, as it was the first time in the history of Davies County that a jury had returned a verdict of guilty of murder in the first degree, and the vote had been unanimous. Continuing on, Judge Stepp polled the jury individually, and each one of the twelve men answered for himself, confirming Mr. Shipley's statement. Standing silently, the courtroom spectators were spellbound, realizing the immensity and seriousness of the occasion.

Minerva watched Ira carefully throughout verdict, and except for the twitching of his right hand as it hung loosely at his side, his manner didn't show that he was upset in any way. Then, looking into the faces of the people in the courtroom, it appeared to Minerva that everyone in the audience was affected more deeply by the jury's decision than was Ira.

Sitting down, Andrew buried his face in his hands. As the family looked toward him, they could see the tears slowly rolling off his fingers and onto the floor as he wept. It was obvious he was crushed, unable to believe this could be happening to his precious son.

James had told Hattie that if the jury found Ira guilty, he would immediately file motions for a new trial and an Arrest of Judgment. But after hearing the verdict, Hattie knew that there was little that could be done now. "This truly is the beginning of the end," she thought wearily. Reaching up to wipe away a tear, an icy feeling passed over her, and as she shivered, she felt like the very breath of Satan had been upon her. Looking skyward, Hattie once again asked the same question that she had asked herself a thousand times before. "How could this have happened?"

The next day, the newspapers wrote that Ira was tried and found guilty by twelve good and lawful men of Davies County. Furthermore, no prisoner had ever received a more fair and impartial trial than he had.

As James had said, he went in the next day and immediately filed motions for a new trial and an Arrest of Judgment. These motions were passed until the following Tuesday, and then were strongly overruled. Afterwards, the courtroom was cleared except for Minerva, Andrew, James, Hattie, and Matthew. Sheriff Sanders kindly stood guard at the door so the family could have a few minutes of privacy with Ira.

Opening his arms to his ailing father, Ira caught Andrew as he fell into them and wept. Except for Andrew's sobs, nothing else could be heard. After a few minutes, Ira held his father's face in his hands and looked lovingly into his eyes. "I'm sorry to have put you through this, Father. Please, let Minerva take you home now."

Touching Ira's face gently, Andrew said between sobs, "I . . . I love you, Boy. I've always loved you."

"I know, Father, now please," he pleaded, "let Minerva take you home."

Compassionately taking Andrew's hand, Minerva led him out of the courthouse to a waiting buggy.

Back inside the courtroom, Ira took Hattie in his arms and begged, "Hattie, please try to keep my father from coming out so much. His health is getting worse, and he needs all the rest that he can get."

"It won't be easy, Ira, he feels, just like the rest of us, that his place is at your side."

"I know, Hattie, but he really needs his rest. Plus, I hate to have him see me locked up in my cell. I'm so embarrassed, and every time he comes, I feel so ashamed. So, please, Hattie, try to keep him away."

Looking at him with sympathy, she said, "All right, Ira, I'll try. What's going to happen next?"

"I believe, Hattie, that I will be sentenced next Monday and without a doubt, be hung."

Hearing a knock at the door, Sheriff Sanders opened it and let Hattie's brothers into the courtroom.

"You best be going, Hattie," Ira said softly, "your brothers are here, and all of you best be getting home."

"Don't worry, Ira, nothing's going to happen to me or your family," Hattie reassured him with confidence. "I've made sure of that. James and I had your family moved to Silver Creek three days ago, and James has hired extra hands to guard the estate until this is all over."

Walking up behind his sister, Robert took Hattie's hand. "Things are getting pretty bad, Hattie. Like Ira said, it would probably be better if we got home." Turning to Ira, his voice got increasingly serious. "I hate to tell you this, Ira, but someone burned your Pa's farm this morning. Both the old house and the new one that Hattie had built are gone, and despite our best efforts, everything was lost. Your Pa really broke down when I told him."

Shocked, Ira fell back against a nearby wall in disbelief. "God," he cried out loudly. "What have I done? My family will never be able to live in Gallatin after this."

Robert's heart swelled as he saw Ira's raw emotions. Hoping to help, he said kindly, "Ira, I'd like to take them to my ranch down in Caldwell County, as soon as. . ." Pausing, the words 'you're hanged' stuck in his throat. "As soon as this is all over."

Gaining his composure, Ira was touched. "I'd appreciate that, Robert. It's obvious my family won't be safe around here anymore, and I really don't want them to have to go through any more heartache."

Hearing the pain in Ira's voice, Hattie and her brothers watched with heavy hearts as the Sheriff took Ira back to his cell.

On their way home, Hattie sat silently beside Matthew, while Shannon drove the carriage. To her amazement, Hattie could occasionally see the sun reflecting off rifles in the distance. Sighing heavily, she knew without a doubt that James's hiring extra men and moving the Saxons to the estate to protect them had been the right thing to do.

The following Monday morning, in accordance with the verdict of the Jury, Ira was brought into court to be sentenced. With everyone present, Judge Stepp calmly repeated the findings of the trial and explained why and how he had come to the decision that would decide Ira's fate.

Looking down at Ira from the bench, the Judge tried to speak as professionally as possible. "Ira Drue Saxon, have you any reason why judgment and sentence should not be pronounced against you according to the law?"

"No, Sir," Ira replied somberly.

Sighing dishearteningly, he began. "Then you leave me no other choice, Ira, but to judge you according to the findings of the trial. Failing in your efforts to get Nicholas Starr to peacefully sign a new will making you his sole beneficiary, you resorted to force. In the scuffle that followed, he started away from you and that is when you decided to rob your friend of his life. You pulled out a gun, and without a second thought, you fired the fatal shots that eventually sent Nicholas Starr to his untimely death. Crawling away like a stray dog in fear of his life, he found a place to hide until it was safe for him to look for help. Luckily for Nick, he found a neighbor and friend to help him. He then made it known shortly before his death that it was you who had precipitated this dastardly crime. And as you stand here today, Ira, you no doubt have some realization of the feelings of Nicholas Starr. For on that fateful day, in the flash of a moment and the twinkling of an eye, all of his earthly hopes and aspirations were taken from him, by shots fired by your own hand."

Showing absolutely no emotion, Ira said nothing but stood motionless, looking only into the face of the judge.

Continuing, the Judge said, "To take the life of another person is a solemn thing, Ira. Even when administered as a penalty to breaking the law, death is nothing to be condoned. Rather it is the ultimate penalty under law for such heinous crimes as the one you have been convicted of. The Bible states very plainly, Ira, that 'thou shalt not kill.' The state of Missouri has done what it could to protect the citizens living within its borders from crimes just like this. We pay out thousands of dollars every year for the education of our youth in order that they might be made intelligent, peaceful, and law-abiding citizens. It seems unthinkable to me that with your having been raised in the loving and kind family in which you were raised, that you would take the life of a friend. It also seems astonishing to me that a young man such as yourself who lived in this community where schoolhouses and churches abound, would be so depraved in your heart as to do such a thing. I doubt there is a man or woman in this courtroom who wouldn't attest to the fact that both of your parents, Samantha and Andrew Saxon, were good, law-abiding citizens and God-fearing people."

Taking a moment to glance at Andrew, the Judge gave him a nod then returned his gaze to Ira. "By your own act have you brought about this condition, and I see you have no one to blame but yourself, Ira. Now that it is too late, you have learned doubtless to your bitter sorrow, that the way of the transgressor is hard. Referring again to the Bible, it is said that 'as a man soweth that shall he also reap.' This shall be literally true in your case. You have sown death, and because of it, you are about to reap death. It only remains for me to pronounce upon you the judgment and sentence of the law, which is death. Therefore, without further delay, I appoint Friday, June 1, 1899, as the day for your execution. The sheriff of this county will safely keep you until that time, when, between the hours of nine o'clock in the forenoon and six o'clock in the afternoon, he will take you to the place prepared for your execution. Then and there he will hang you by the neck until you are dead. It is up to you to make your own reconciliation and peace with God, may He have mercy upon your soul."

Hearing the gavel slam, Hattie's blood ran cold. It was now official. Ira would hang, and nothing, it appeared, could stop it.

As Ira stood in silence, his sisters, Mary and Emily, could only hang their heads in despair. For months they had hoped that some sort of evidence would surface that could prove Ira's innocence, but now, with the date for the execution set, they knew the time for hope was over. The end was in sight, and unless a miracle occurred, Ira would be dead in three months. Walking hand in hand, they left the courtroom with the rest of Hattie's family, leaving only Matthew and Hattie alone with Ira to contemplate the events that had just transpired. Turning slowly to face Hattie, tears streamed freely down

Ira's weary face. Embracing each other tenderly, their embrace wasn't an embrace of lovers, as during the long months of his imprisonment their relationship had changed considerably. Instead, it was an embrace of friends who had been through a lot together.

Very frustrated, Hattie hated the way things had turned out. Looking up at Ira, she said, "I just can't believe you let it come to this. Why in the world didn't you make a greater effort to prove your innocence?" Receiving no response, she added, "James begged you to take the stand, yet you wouldn't do it. Why? Who are you protecting?"

Still ignoring her questions, Ira stared down at the ground in silence. Then, looking up, he changed the subject. "How's my Pa?"

"Since the farmhouse was burned, he's gotten worse every day. Mary, Emily, and Hunter seldom leave him, and they are really worried that he won't last much longer." Pausing, she could see the anguish in his eyes. "He wants to come to town to visit you, Ira. I've tried to keep him away like you asked, but he is getting very anxious to see you. He says his place is with you, and it has been killing him to be away so much. Sheriff Sanders said we could bring a big chair to your cell at the jail and make him as comfortable as possible, if you'll agree."

Resigned to his fate, he turned to Matthew and asked, "What do you think I should do, Matt?"

"Your father is ill, Ira, very ill. I honestly believe you should see him." Shaking his head, his words were firm. "I wouldn't postpone it if I were you because the way it is looking, you may not get another opportunity." Nodding, Ira agreed.

Later that evening, Matthew and Robert pulled up in front of the mansion in a carriage. As Robert waited patiently, Matthew went in, got Andrew, and carried him through the big front doors of the house and placed him in the carriage. Inside the carriage, Mary and Emily sat on either side of him in an effort to make him as comfortable as possible. Hattie stayed behind with Cameron and the family, so that Ira could spend some time alone with his father. Driving away, eight gunmen fell in alongside the carriage as they rode into town, just in case.

They arrived at the jail to find both the Sheriff and his wife waiting for them. The Sheriff had brought in a comfortable chair and footstool and had it placed in Ira's cell for the ailing old gentleman, who had once been a constable in the county himself. Matthew carried Andrew inside in his strong arms, as easily as a father would carry his sleeping child. The kindly old man had lost fifty pounds during his illness and was now only a slight figure of the man he once had been.

After several months of Ira proving that he was trustworthy, the Sheriff left Ira's cell door open, hoping that it would take away the harshness of the jail for Andrew.

All the way into town, Andrew had promised himself that he would make this visit as uplifting to Ira as he could, and as he entered the jail in Matthew's arms, he bore a big smile. Crying out in joy, Andrew said, "There's my boy!"

Ira, standing just inside the door, took his father from Matthew's arms, then thanked Matthew and Robert for their remarkable kindness.

Smiling, Matthew responded with his patented smile, "It was nothing, Ira. We were just glad to be of some help. We're going to go over to Doc Cowley's for a spell to give you some privacy, but we'll be back to check on you in awhile."

After everyone left, Ira stood rocking his father gently in his arms. Laughing, he said, "Well, Pa, it looks like life has come full circle. Instead of you holding me in your arms, I'm holding you in mine."

Smiling, Andrew gave Ira a once over. "Looks like Mrs. Sanders is feedin' you really well. I believe you've actually picked up some weight durin' your stay here."

"That I have, Pa. She's an excellent cook, and she and the Sheriff treat me like I am their own son." Holding his father at arms length, Ira couldn't believe how tiny his father had become. "It looks to me like you're losing too much weight. Why, if a stiff breeze came through here, I think it would blow you away."

Placing his father in the chair, Ira wrapped him carefully in a heavy blanket. "All joking aside, Pa, I'm very worried about you."

"You needn't be, Son. I'm in God's hands now, just as you are. And your Mama is patiently waitin' for both of us."

Ira, hearing his father's kind words, couldn't contain his emotions any longer and suddenly broke down at the mention of his mother. Falling to his knees, he laid his head in his father's lap and began to cry. Sheriff Sanders, caught up in this tender scene, stood spellbound as he fought to contain his own emotions.

Stroking his son's hair lovingly, Andrew's voice quivered as he spoke. "I know you got a rotten deal, Son. It's obvious that someone not only wants you out of the way, but they want you dead. I don't care what the newspapers wrote. You didn't get an honest trial. That damn Stanley Johnson is as crooked as a river windin' its way to the sea. Just seein' the smugness on his face the day the verdict was announced made me want to strangle him. He, along with that no good jury they picked, had it out for you from the beginnin'. Now, I don't have any proof one way or the other, but the word about town is that someone paid handsomely to see you get the death penalty, and after seein' the way thin's played out, I agree whole-heartedly. I just wish there was somethin' I could do to help you, Son."

"Pa, you've always done your best to help me."

"I'm afraid, Boy, that I ain't gonna live long. If I don't, I'll be right there with your Mama when you come into heaven." Pausing, Andrew touched Ira's cheek. "You hold on to this one thought, Son. No matter how terrible it may seem, even at the last, I promise you that the moment it's over, you'll be in the arms of your Mama and me, and nobody will ever hurt you again."

As Ira sobbed uncontrollably, Andrew continued stroking his son's head and, like any good father, cried with him. With hot tears staining the side of Andrew's worn, wrinkled face, his memory raced back through time to the day Ira was born. Ira's birth had been the most difficult of all the children born to his beloved Samantha because he was a breach birth. But when the doctor finally delivered him, Andrew took Ira gently in his arms and instantly fell in love with him. He knew in that moment that they were kindred spirits and were meant to be father and son.

Then, in an instant, Andrew's mind raced forward to Ira's fourth birthday, when he presented him with a small pony. At eleven, he had taken him to a tent meeting, and Ira was 'saved'. Not long after that he was taught to shoot. Finally, when he was fifteen and taller than his father, he and the other children faced the untimely death of their mother, Samantha. Andrew could still hear Ira's well-developed baritone voice as he stood at the end of his mother's casket, singing her favorite hymn. Looking down at Ira now, Andrew couldn't help but think, "How could my precious son's life come to this?

At twenty-two years old, his life has hardly even begun. Just married such a short time to Miss Hattie, and now falsely accused of the murder of his friend. Where, oh Lord, is the justice of it all?"

"Pa," Ira said quietly, "I'm afraid I'll never make it to Heaven. I didn't kill Nick, but I have done things that will definitely keep me from passing through the pearly gates."

"Why, Son? What have you done?"

Pausing for several moments, Ira's shame was almost more than he could handle. "My life is in such a mess, Pa, that I can't talk about it, but I won't go to Heaven, I assure you. It's not your fault or Mama's. You raised me right, but along the way, I simply fell in with the wrong people, which caused me to make a lot of wrong choices. Actually, they were terrible choices, made because I felt alone and lonely. Some things that I have done, Pa, I'm afraid are unforgivable." Choking on his last words, he again laid his head on his father's lap, and together, they were silent for some time.

Seeing them holding each other quietly, the Sheriff left the jail, only to return a few minutes later with coffee and pie. Speaking softly, he said, "The wife felt that some hot coffee and pie might be just the thin' on a cool night." Offering it to them, Ira took it graciously.

"Sheriff," Andrew asked, "If you'd permit it, I'd like to spend the night here with my boy."

"Ain't any rule against it, Andrew, but I'm afraid it won't be very comfortable for you in that chair."

"If I can just sit here and hold my boy like this through the night, I'll be just fine. I really don't want to leave him tonight. Surely you can understand that, can't you?"

Nodding his head, he replied, "Anythin' you want, Andrew."

"Ira tells me that you and your wife have treated him like one of your own. I want you to know, as his Pa, how deeply I appreciate all the kindness you've shown him."

Smiling, the Sheriff nodded and then left them alone. An hour later, Matthew returned with Ira's sisters, and deciding to stay the night with Ira and Andrew, he sent them home with Robert. Visiting quietly with the Sheriff, he was told that Ira had been a model prisoner and a complete gentleman during his incarceration.

Sitting where he could see Ira, Matthew observed him sitting on the floor with his head in his father's lap and Andrew stroking his heavy dark hair. It was a truly peaceful sight, and throughout the night, they didn't leave each other's side.

The next morning, Matthew was awakened by Ira's sobs. Silently, he wondered if Ira had cried all night. Standing and walking to him, Matthew reached down and patted his shoulder.

Turning to look up at him, tears rolled freely down Ira's face. "My Pa must have passed away in the night, Matt. I fell asleep with my head in his lap, and when I woke up, he was gone."

Reaching down, Matthew felt the old man's neck for a pulse, while the Sheriff came to them with a mirror and placed it below his nostrils for some sign of breathing. But after their best efforts to prove otherwise, Ira was right. Andrew had died in the night.

Hearing a knock at the door, the Sheriff opened it and Shannon and Robert entered. Hearing from Matthew that Andrew had died, Shannon said to Ira, "You're a lucky man, Ira, to have had your Pa all those years. Robert and I would have given anything if our Pa had been as loving and kind to us as Andrew was with you."

Sighing heavily, Ira knew they were right. Looking skyward, he thanked God for the blessing of having his father die in peace at his side, and with tears in his eyes, he was in awe of God's mercy.

Within the hour, the undertaker, Mr. Scarborough, was called, and Robert accompanied Andrew's body to the funeral parlor. Matthew, knowing the family needed to be informed, sent Shannon to Silver Creek, while he remained with Ira to console him. Ira paced back and forth in his cell, and not until Hattie arrived with his rest of his family, did he finally settle down. Calling the Sheriff to his cell, he reached through the bars and took his hands. "Thank you, Sheriff, from the bottom of my heart for letting my Pa stay with me last night. It meant everything to me, and I think I can face things now."

* * *

THE WEATHER COULDN'T POSSIBLY have been worse than it was on the day of Andrew's funeral. It rained continually, and there were extremely strong winds. The thunder rolled incessantly, and so heavily that it literally shook a person's insides to the very core of their being.

Judge Stepp, having an understanding heart, gave special permission for Ira to be transported to the gravesite at Silver Creek, under heavy guard by Sheriff Sanders and twenty-four deputies.

Standing at the end of his father's grave in shackles, Ira was chained to Hattie's wrist for added protection. Standing motionless, the cold, biting wind whipped about her legs, blowing her cape open several times, while everyone else huddled closely together in an effort to protect themselves from the wind.

Speaking to the Judge, who was standing next to her, Minerva commented sadly, "What a pathetic scene this is for the God of heaven and the angels to look upon, Judge." Pulling his coat tighter, the Judge agreed.

Stepping forward, James prayed aloud. "Dear Father in heaven, we are here for a most solemn occasion. We ask Thee in the most humble of spirits to please temper the elements until we can lay to rest Thy dear son, Andrew."

To everyone's amazement, as he concluded his prayer, the clouds rolled away, the wind ceased, and the sun shined down upon Andrew's family and friends. Those who stood at the gravesite marveled, but Hattie, knowing what a faithful man James was, wasn't surprised at all that God would grant him an answer to his prayer in such an obvious and miraculous way.

Stepping up to the casket, Reverend Walker gave a wonderful eulogy, and once he was finished, he turned to Ira and said, "Just a few days ago your father called me to the estate, Ira. He was aware of the seriousness of his illness and said that he doubted he would live much longer. It was his request that I ask you and Miss Hattie to sing his favorite hymn today. Would you be up to it?"

Standing quietly, the Reverend's words were hard for Ira to accept. After several moments of silence, tears began to form in Ira's eyes and he said to the crowd with a solemn voice, "Oh, how dearly I love my Pa." Thinking to himself about all his sins, though, Ira couldn't help but think that he would never see his Pa again, not in this life or in the life to come. Hanging his head, he said under his breath, "I have no hope."

Reverend Walker, seeing that Ira's mind was preoccupied, asked again. "Ira, would you and Miss Hattie sing your father's favorite hymn?"

Nodding wearily, Ira cleared his throat and whispered quietly to Hattie, "Will you join me?"

"Yes," she replied lovingly. And after they took their places in front of the crowd, they poured out their souls in song. Ira in particular sang with the deepest of emotions, his voice carrying through the little cemetery and across the barren winter fields, to the great throng of people gathered along the road. Andrew Saxon had always been a good and honest man respected by all who knew him, and when Ira reached the last stanza and Hattie's voice joined his, there was no greater, nor more fitting, tribute they could have given his father.

After Ira and Hattie finished singing, Reverend Walker tried to comfort Ira and pulling his head down close to him, whispered in his ear. "Remember, Ira, the scriptures say 'though your sins be as scarlet'."

Knowing the passage, Ira hung his head and replied, "I know, Reverend. I know."

Making their way back to the mansion, everyone was again amazed as the clouds rolled back in, and the wind picked up. Watching Andrew's casket being lowered and the grave filled, Hattie was taken back in amazement as the very moment the last shovel of dirt fell on Andrew's grave, the heavens opened and there was a torrential downpour.

Having suffered so much pain over the past two years, Hattie knew that without question her life with Ira was coming to an end. Seeing the Sheriff taking him back to the jail, her heart was heavy, knowing his hanging would come much too soon. "How could my life have come to this?" she thought exasperated. "A second tragic marriage in such a short time?" Knowing that things would only get worse before they could get better, she retired that night and prayed for the courage and ability to cope with the hard times that most assuredly awaited her in the months ahead.

Chapter 8
MORE THAN MEETS THE EYE

IN THE MONTHS LEADING UP to Ira's hanging, James filed motion after motion with Judge Stepp, desperately hoping for a stay of execution. James, like Matthew and Hattie, felt that Ira had been framed. Together, all three felt that Abner, Jess, and Newton along with Laville had somehow had something to do with Nick's death, but despite their strong feelings on the subject, they knew that unless a stay of execution was granted they would never have enough time to find out what really happened.

Standing before the judge a mere three weeks before the hanging, James was near his wits end. Looking over his shoulder at Hattie and Matthew, he knew time was running out. His voice trembled as he approached the bench. "Please, Judge," James said earnestly, hoping to appeal to his softer side. "All I am asking for is a sufficient amount of time to look for evidence that can prove my client's innocence."

Sighing heavily, Judge Stepp shook his head. "Mr. Kinnion, we have gone over this time and time again. You have had over five months to thoroughly go through every detail of this case. I simply don't see how granting you any more time could help. In my professional opinion, if there was any major evidence to be found, it would have been found by now."

Stepping closer to the bench, James wasn't about to give up that easily. "Granted, Judge, we have had a lot of time already, but in my defense, your honor, I am only one man. For the first couple of months, I ran myself ragged trying to put together a solid defense for the trial, and then, after the sentencing and even up until this very day, the majority of my time has been spent in and around this court-house filing papers trying to buy my client more time. That is time that I could have and should have been spending out looking for the key suspects that I couldn't find before Ira's trial."

"Oh yes, these key suspects you keep talking about. All right, Mr. Kinnion, I give. Just who are these 'key' suspects you keep talk-ing about?"

"Well, Your Honor, I have very good reason to believe that there are people out there who know the truth about that fateful night last November, but because I have been so busy, I have not been able to orchestrate the type of investigation that I feel would be required to find them. Don't get me wrong, Judge, I have had investigators searching around locally since the beginning, but as I'm sure you know, it is rather hard to find someone who doesn't want to be found. And the few people that I feel know the truth about that night have, I'm afraid, gone to great lengths to keep themselves hid-den."

"You still haven't answered my question, Mr. Kinnion. Who ex-actly are you looking for?"

"Jess and Abner Garland and Miss Hattie's Pa, Newton."

Leaning forward slowly, the Judge knew all too well how devious those three men could be. Staring straight ahead, his mind raced back to the night at Silver Creek when Abner and Jess swore vengeance on Hattie and her family after Rebecca had forced them to sign the papers disinheriting themselves from her fortune. Chills had run down his spine that night, and now, hearing James mention them, the Judge again felt an eerie chill. Clearing his throat, his tone changed significantly. Speaking receptively, he asked, "So, what exactly do you want to do?"

Taking a deep breath, James was relieved to see the Judge's demeanor softening. Glancing back at Hattie with a slight smile, he continued. "Well, with your permission, Judge, Hattie and I would like to hire an extensive group of private investigators to search out these people so that we can question them. We will search the entire country if need be, but as you can surely see, it will take awhile. The only reason we haven't commenced with this type of search up until now is because we wanted to make sure we had sufficient time to compile our findings before the hanging." Looking up at the Judge pleadingly, James let out a ragged breath. "I guess you could say we didn't want to be looking over our shoulders hoping that we had enough time. That is why I have repeatedly come before you hoping that I could receive a stay of execution. Now, I know it is not standard procedure to postpone a hanging, but given the circumstances of this case, I hope you will seriously consider our proposal."

Leaning back in his chair, Judge Stepp rubbed his chin gently. It was obvious he was deep in thought, and after what seemed like an eternity to Hattie, he sighed heavily, again leaned forward in his chair, and placed his elbows squarely on the oak bench. "Six months," he said firmly. "I will give you six months to conduct your research and collect your findings." Turning to Hattie, he said, "It is only because of how highly I regard you, Miss Hattie, that am willing to agree to this. I wish you nothing but the best, but be forewarned," he said somberly, "if you do not find anything, Ira's execution will com-

mence expeditiously." With that, the Judge banged his gavel and retired to his chambers.

Looking skyward, Hattie was overcome with relief. The delay
was her first real glimmer of hope. She now knew that they would
have the time necessary to conduct a real search for Abner, Jess, and
Newton. Embracing James, she asked pointedly, "How soon can
you have the investigators ready to go?"

Giving her a glittery smile, he replied, "They will be on the case
tomorrow."

* * *

WITH SEVERAL OF THE BEST INVESTIGATORS in the
country now on the case, Hattie was extremely hopeful that they
would find some answers. Clinging to her faith, she believed that
somehow the truth would prevail before it was too late. Waiting patiently, the weeks rolled on with no major findings until finally, in
mid July, one of the investigators found something.

Jacob Jones was a big city investigator from Chicago, and riding
up to the estate in the summer sun, he bore a big smile. He was one
of the first people James had hired and was widely considered the
best investigator in the Midwest, if not the country.

Seeing him riding up, Hattie and Matthew went out to meet him,
and after exchanging pleasantries, they anxiously escorted him into
the parlor where Mary already had iced tea waiting for them. Having
him take a seat, Hattie was elated. "Okay, Mr. Jones, spill the beans.
What did you find?"

Smiling, Jacob replied, "I take it you received my telegram."

"Yes, we sure did, Mr. Jones, and I must say that you have definitely
gotten our attention," Matthew responded respectfully. "We are most
anxious to hear about the information that you have on Newton."

Looking around, Jacob asked, "Where is Mr. Kinnion?"

"Oh, he is on business at the Capitol right now, Mr. Jones," Hattie answered quickly. "But don't worry about his absence. I assure you that I keep him abreast of everything that is going on by telegram." Turning, Hattie pulled up a chair, and as she sat down, she entreated, "Please, don't keep us in suspense. Tell us what you found."

"First of all, I want to say that this has been a very interesting case. I spent weeks looking high and low with no real results until one day I ran into a person who had seen someone matching Newton's description in Keokuk, Iowa. So, with great haste, I made my way there nurturing high hopes, and I must say that I was not disappointed." Glancing at both Matthew and Hattie, he could see they were hanging on his every word. "It turns out," he continued, "that Newton has a very large parcel of land right on the outskirts of town. Six hundred acres to be exact and right in the middle of this prime farmland is a house fit for a king. Believe me when I tell you that he is doing just fine."

Hattie couldn't believe her ears. "How could Pa have all this wealth in Iowa?" she thought bewildered. "In all the years that we lived on the farm, we never had a dime to spare." Wanting answers, she asked, "Are you sure it was my Pa, Mr. Jones? Because as far as I know, he didn't have much when he left town?"

"I'm sure," he reassured her with confidence. "I followed him several times to make sure, and though he went by the name of Newton Anthony, I'm positive it was your Pa."

Hearing the name of Anthony, Hattie knew immediately Jacob was telling the truth. Looking over at Matthew, her voice was weak. "Anthony is Pa's middle name."

Walking to her side, Matthew offered her his hand for support, and directing his attention at Jacob, he asked, "What else did you see when you were following Newton?"

"Well, surprisingly enough, around Keokuk he is known as a pillar of society. He attends church regularly, donates money for town projects, and is generally well liked and respected. It appeared as if he was an entirely different person than the one that Mr. Kinnion described." Taking a deep breath, he paused momentarily. Then, after taking a sip of the tea that Mary had poured him, he added, "But don't get me wrong, that was just what he appeared to be. Unbeknownst to the people of Keokuk, he leads a secret life, running off to saloons in surrounding towns quite often. I followed him on a couple of these excursions, and when I did, I saw him meet with two men who fit Abner and Jess Garland's descriptions exactly. I was never able to get close enough to hear what they were discussing, but I am positive that it was the Garlands that Newton was meeting with."

Standing up, Hattie's shock had now turned to rage. "I knew it! Those three are still in cahoots, even after all this time. Matthew, get Cameron, Dakota, and the men ready. We're going to Keokuk. I want to confront that good for nothing SOB face to face." Pacing back and forth, she added, "I just know that he knows who killed Nick."

Grabbing Matthew's arm as he was about to leave, Jacob urged him to wait. Standing before them, he took a deep breath. "Before either of you go running off to Keokuk, there is one more thing that I haven't mentioned yet."

Turning to face Jacob, Hattie could tell by the look in his eyes that what he was about to say was very serious. Sighing, she closed her eyes and thought, "What now?"

"I would rather not go into details, as it is something very personal, and I don't feel that I am the one who should tell you this," he stated solemnly. "Instead, I think it would be better if you found out on your own. Rest assured, though, that Newton is not the man you think he is by any stretch of the imagination. He truly has a whole other life in Keokuk."

Silently, Hattie wondered what on earth was so personal about her Pa that Jacob wouldn't tell them the rest of what he found. It seemed very odd to her, but before she could question Jacob further, he said, "I'd like to stay longer, but I have many other engagements." Walking over to Hattie, he placed his hand on her shoulder. "I know you would like more details, Miss Hattie, but trust me, when you find out what your Pa has been up to you will understand my not wanting to tell you."

"How will we know exactly where his farm is?" Matthew questioned politely.

"It is about a mile outside the north side of town," he responded. Then, as he walked quickly to the door, he added, "Believe me, you can't miss it." Opening the door, he looked back once more and said, "It has been a pleasure working for you, Miss Hattie, and if you or James need any more help, feel free to contact me." Stepping out into the hallway, he gave a final smile, tipped his hat, and was speedily on his way.

Dumbfounded, Hattie stood motionless looking out the window for several minutes, mulling over Jacob's haunting words. Finally, as she felt Matthew put his arms around her, she said with a concerned tone, "Matthew, is it just me, or did Jacob's unwillingness to tell us the rest of the details about Pa bother you as well?"

"It was kind of odd, yes, but I'm sure he had his reasons." Turning her around to face him, he gave her loving smile, hoping to calm her. "Besides, we will find out soon enough. I'll tell Cameron and the other men to pack their bags, and we can leave early tomorrow morning. Whatever it is, I'm sure that we can handle it. It's not like this family isn't used to the abnormal. Heck, one of things I love most about this job is I never know what's going to happen from one day to the next." Flashing his glittery smile once more, Hattie couldn't help but feel better.

Pulling him closer to her, she wanted very much to believe what he was saying was true, but deep down, she knew there was a lot more to Jacob's secrecy than met the eye."

Chapter 9
CHARLATAN

AFTER TALKING TO MINERVA, Rebecca, and Lou the next morning, Hattie and Dakota were ready to leave for Keokuk. Rebecca and Lou extended nothing but good wishes regarding their trip, but deep down, Lou was crushed that she couldn't go along for support. She had already promised Rebecca that she would accompany her to Richmond, and they were due to leave at the end of the week.

Seeing her daughters so determined to find and confront Newton, Minerva worried about their safety, but after talking at length with Hattie in private, she reluctantly agreed.

Hattie left strict instructions with Minerva that if she didn't hear from them each day by wire, James was to be notified immediately of their last location.

Watching George load the buggy bound for the train station, Minerva kissed Hattie one last time and said, "At least I'll have some comfort knowing you're safe with Matthew, Cameron, and your entourage traveling with you."

Embracing her mother, Hattie smiled. "Exactly, Mother, so don't worry. We'll be home before you know it, and with any luck, we'll have some answers."

Within minutes, Matthew took his place in the buggy, and taking the reins, he led them down the road. Giving Hattie a wink, he said,

"You and Dakota will look less conspicuous, Hattie, if Cameron and I travel as your husbands. The rest of the men can travel with us, but individually, causing less attention."

Nodding her head, Hattie was in total agreement, and from the moment they reached the train station, they did just that.

The trip itself was uneventful and pleasant. Then, shortly after getting settled in a local hotel, Hattie and Dakota decided to it was time to find their father. On their way out of the hotel, they stopped momentarily to talk to the manager. Without giving him too much information, Hattie told him that they were looking for a man named Newton Anthony. The manager was very helpful and confirmed what Jacob had said about her father. At the conclusion of their discussion, the manager even went out of his way to give them detailed directions to his estate.

Riding out of town to the north, they were shocked at what they saw. Even though they had been told that Newton had acquired a great deal of wealth, they simply could not believe their eyes. For sprawled out before them was a very large and spacious home surrounded by hundreds of acres of fertile farmland said by the hotel manager to belong to Newton. Sitting quietly in the buggy, Hattie thought to herself, "What kind of a man is Pa, to have had all of this wealth here in Keokuk, yet force us to live like paupers in Missouri." Fuming inside, she remembered what the hotel manager had said. He told her that the man he knew as Newton Anthony, had come to town almost twelve years ago with a great deal of money. He bought a beautiful home and six hundred acres of land and had been an outstanding citizen ever since.

Leaving her men all along the main road, Hattie, Matthew, Cameron, and Dakota rode up to the house alone. As Matthew stopped the buggy in front of the house, Hattie looked in amazement over the beautifully manicured yard and large two-story house. "One thing is for sure," she said to Dakota, "If this is Pa's house, he's got someone to help him take care of it, because I've never know him to keep anything this well-kept. Heck," she said jokingly, "Mama couldn't even get him to keep the lawn cut at our farm. Shannon and the older boys always had to do it."

As the four of them got out and walked up the front steps, a very pleasant woman met them at the door. Her appearance caught Hattie off guard, but after looking her over and seeing her wearing an apron, she concluded that she must be the housemaid.

Looking directly into Matthew's handsome face, the lady smiled and said, "Hello, Gentlemen, young Ladies, how may I help you?"

Smiling back, Matthew answered kindly, "We're here to see Mr. Anthony, Ma'am."

Bewildered, the woman responded, "Okay, who shall I say is calling?"

"We'd rather announce ourselves, if you don't mind," Hattie said as politely as she could. "We've traveled a very great distance to speak with him, and we'd like for it to be a surprise. May we please come in?"

The woman, still puzzled, politely refused, looking to Matthew for an explanation.

Matthew, always keeping his cool, spoke in a voice as smooth as silk. "I know this may seem like an unusual request, and I can see that we've caught you by surprise. We were hoping you would let us meet with Mr. Anthony without going into a lot of detail, but as you appear to be a very astute woman, I suppose we must tell you why we're here. The truth is these two young ladies are sisters." Pointing

first to Hattie, he said, "This is Mrs. Hattie Saxon," and then, pointing to Dakota, he added, "and this is Mrs. Dakota Kinnion. We've
traveled from Gallatin, Missouri, in search of their father, and we
have reason to believe that Mr. Anthony is that person."

Flustered, the lady turned again and looked at Hattie. The color
of Hattie's red hair disturbed her greatly, but despite Matthew's
smooth words, she held firm on not letting them in. "Oh, you must
be mistaken. My husband has no children, other than our two
daughters and our son, Newton, Jr. He's never been married before,
I assure you."

Hearing the lady's statement, Hattie's mouth dropped. She
couldn't believe what she had just heard. The words 'my husband'
ran over and over in her mind, as she stood dumbfounded. "Did I
just hear what I thought I heard," she thought frantically. Looking
at Dakota, Matthew, and Cameron, she could tell that they just as
shocked as she was. Shaking her head in disbelief, she stammered,
"I'm sorry, Ma'am, did you just say your . . . husband?"

"Yes, I did," she replied bluntly. "My name is Lorna Anthony,
and I am Newton's wife."

Standing silent for several moments, this was the last thing Hattie
had expected, but at the same time, somehow, she wasn't surprised
to find out her Pa had been living a secret life. All of the unexplained
absences now made sense. He had been with this woman, his second
wife, in Iowa. Then, remembering back to what Jacob said about
there being more that he didn't want to tell her, she now understood
the reason for his secrecy, and looking into the eyes of this sweet-
looking woman, Hattie thought, "I wouldn't have wanted to be the
bearer of this type of bad news either."

As everything began to come together in her mind, Hattie inwardly fumed with anger. "Of all the lowdown rotten things Pa has done in his life," she thought to herself, "this has got to take the cake." Taking a deep breath, she realized that they were getting nowhere standing on the porch, and gaining her wits about her, she tried to come up with a plan. Thinking fast, she said, "Perhaps you're right, Ma'am. You see, we've been searching for our father for months now, and meeting your, uh, husband was, well, our last hope. We're so sorry to have troubled you, and we're not here to cause any problems, I assure you. It is just that our father was last seen here in Keokuk, and couple that with the fact that your husband evidently resembles him very much, we hoped to at least meet Mr. Anthony." Looking at Lorna with her beautiful green eyes, Hattie pleaded, "Please, Ma'am, would you please let us see him?"

Seeing the sincerity in Hattie's eyes and hearing the kindness in her voice, Lorna's heart melted. She had always been tenderhearted, and though it was not normal for her to invite strangers into the house, she decided to make an exception for Hattie. Smiling, Lorna said, "I was in the middle of preparing lunch, but I guess the very least I can do is to introduce you to Newton. He's in the parlor reading. If you will follow me, I'll take you there."

Relieved that Lorna had agreed to let them in, Hattie, Dakota, Matthew, and Cameron quietly followed her down the hallway toward the parlor. As they walked, Hattie admired the lovely paintings that adorned the walls of the well-furnished home.

Reaching the parlor, Mrs. Anthony quietly opened doors, revealing exactly what Hattie had been told she would find, for there, in a chair across the room, sat her father. He was reading, yet Hattie had never known him to just sit and read anything. He appeared deep in thought and was completely caught off guard when Hattie, without giving Mrs. Anthony an opportunity to introduce them, called out, "Pa, Mama said it's time for dinner, better shake a leg."

The element of surprise was just as Hattie had hoped, as the sound of her voice was so familiar to Newton that, without looking up, he answered, "In a minute, Hattie." Then, suddenly realizing what he had said, he dropped the book he was reading into his lap and looked up, startled to see Hattie, Dakota, Matthew, and Cameron standing on either side of Lorna.

Shocked at Newton's response, Lorna took a step in his direction and spoke with grave concern. "Newton, you told me you were never married! Yet you answered this young lady by the very same name that she was introduced to me as! What's the meaning of this?"

Refusing to answer Lorna, he glared at Hattie and Dakota. "Just what in the hell do you two think you're doing here?"

"I'd show a little respect, if I were you, Mr. Morran," insisted Matthew.

Lorna stood in disbelief at what she was hearing, as Newton responded coldly, "You, Matt, can shut the hell up!"

Dakota, angry beyond comprehension, stepped forward toward the sound of her father's voice. "Pa, what the hell are you doing married to this woman when you're still married to Mama?"

Lorna's shock was now turning to anger. Stepping in front of Hattie and looking Newton squarely in the face, she said firmly, "Newton, I asked you a question, and I expect an answer! What is the meaning of all this?"

Trying to do damage control, Newton took Lorna by the hand. "Please go upstairs, Lorna. This doesn't concern you." Then, glancing in Hattie's direction, he added spitefully, "I will handle these people."

Yanking her hand away from him, Lorna was furious. "Don't you dare tell me to go upstairs, Newton. I am not a child, and I intend to get to the bottom of this. These people, as you call them, say they are your children, and by the way you have so harshly responded to them, I am beginning to believe them." Turning to Hattie, she asked, "Mrs. Saxon, how long have you been searching for Newton?"

"A very long time, Ma'am. And his name isn't Newton Anthony, it's Newton Anthony Morran."

Frowning, Lorna walked angrily to a large window that overlooked Newton's expansive farmland. Gazing outside, she asked, "How many children are there in your family?"

"My parents had seven sons, three daughters, and three children that didn't survive infancy. Plus, I have come to find that he has a daughter about my age somewhere in Texas by a woman named Lucille Devereaux."

Glaring at Hattie, Newton wanted to kill her. "How dare they come here and mess up what I've worked so hard all these years to build," he thought.

"And your mother, is she still living?" Lorna asked, still not turning around.

"Yes, Ma'am, she was busy baking pies when Dakota Jayne and I left Gallatin last week."

"That's quite enough, Hattie!" Newton shouted, as he stepped toward her. "You and Dakota Jayne can take Matthew and Cameron and leave now; I believe you've caused enough trouble for one day!"

Backing away from her Father, Hattie was astonished to see him dressed in clothes befitting a gentleman. Hearing him walk toward them, Dakota turned in the direction of his footsteps and asked pointedly, "What has happened to the way you speak, Pa? You don't sound at all like you did at home."

"I, like yourself, Dakota, have learned to speak properly."

Turning from the window, Lorna couldn't understand his reply. "Why, Newton, you have always spoken like this, what are you talking about?" With all that was happening, her mind was reeling. This man that she had married, loved, and had three children with was scaring her. "What kind of an imposter is he?" she thought frantically. "How could this man, my husband, be a bigamist? God," she pleaded in her mind, "what more don't I know?"

Focusing back on the conversation Newton was having with Hattie and Dakota, Lorna listened in amazement as he continued to argue with them. "Could it be," she thought, "that these two beautiful young women are his daughters." Listening to the heated words, there was little doubt that they were, as they knew too much about Newton for it to be a coincidence. "Besides," she told herself, "what possible reason would they have to lie?" Looking up and seeing Newton get even closer to Hattie, Lorna hurried directly in front of her and confronted her husband. "I want some straight answers, Newton, and I want them now! Just what is the meaning of this charade?"

Not saying a word, Newton was seething. His anger, boiling up inside of him, was turning to rage. He turned away from Lorna without giving her an answer and returned to his chair, where he had been sitting when they had entered the room. Standing over it in silence, he looked out of the nearby window and across his fields, trying to decide exactly what it was he was going to say.

Waiting for Newton to answer, the room had fallen deathly silent. After a minute, Lorna invited Hattie and Dakota to sit and be patient. Then, hoping to calm him down, she joined Newton by his chair, but still, he said nothing, his face full of anger.

Lorna, a kind, gentle, patient woman, could not for the life of her understand why the man she loved so dearly had lied to her from the very beginning. In all the years they had been married, which were close to twelve now, he had never shown her or their three children anything other than love, understanding, and kindness. His manner had been gracious and he portrayed himself as a man of honor and a perfect gentleman. As she looked at him now, she wondered if she was completely crazy. Was Newton really nothing more than a 'charlatan'? Was his whole life with her just an act? It was difficult to believe, yet the overwhelming evidence was beginning to tip the scales in that direction."

Trying to remain calm, she touched his arm and entreated, "Please, Newton, I'm waiting for some answers."

Hattie, holding Dakota's hand, looked up at Matthew, smiled, and winked. "We've got him now," she said triumphantly, just above a whisper.

Looking down at Lorna, Newton's eyes narrowed, grew cold, and once again he turned away.

Shuddering slightly, Lorna took a step back. This was positively not the man she knew. Her thoughts raced back through the hallways of her mind to the day she first met him in Keokuk. They had both entered the bank at the same time, and opening the door for her, he graciously stepped aside then followed her inside. They spoke momentarily then standing behind her, he waited as she made a transaction with the teller. Afterwards, she walked to the bank president and could feel his eyes following her.

As Newton opened a sizeable account that day, he overheard the bank president mention her late husband's name, indicating she was a widow.

After finishing her conversation with the bank president, Lorna stepped aside as this tall, handsome gentleman introduced himself as Mr. Newton Anthony. She thought to herself, at that time, how handsomely dressed he was and how well he carried himself. Listening to him speaking, she surmised that he was a gentleman. After introductions, he took her hand and shook it gently. She noticed his eyes had a certain sparkle to them, his teeth were straight and white, and his smile was warm and friendly.

In the weeks that followed, they met often in church, and Newton made it a habit to sit with her. During the eighth week, he asked her to marry him, and as a wedding gift, he presented her with their beautiful home and six hundred acres of land that surrounded it. He took great pains to explain to her before they were married that it was necessary that he travel quite often. He said that he had business interests in Des Moines and Kansas City, as well as Chicago, and they would require that he be gone for extended periods of times, several times a year. She was quite lonely until they began having a family, but when Newton was at home, everything was glorious. Their family life was beautiful, and she deeply appreciated the fact that he had seen to it that financially she wanted for nothing. But now, that same man who she loved so dear stood before her, a total stranger.

Turning around slowly, he looked at Lorna again, this time his face was expressionless. In a commanding tone, he said, "Go upstairs, Lorna. We'll talk about this when I've finished with these people."

Much to his surprise, Lorna didn't budge. "Don't use that tone of voice with me. Just who do you think you're talking to, Newton? It's perfectly evident these two lovely ladies are your daughters. It is also obvious that I most certainly am not legally your wife, as you already have a wife in Missouri." Leaving him at the window, Lorna walked to Hattie and stood beside her. "Now, Newton, your daughters and I have asked you several questions, we want some straight answers, and we want them, now." Newton started to raise his voice, but decided against it when he saw Matthew and Cameron step forward. Continuing, Lorna asked, "Newton, are you legally married to their mother?"

"Yes," he replied coldly.

Inwardly devastated, finally having the truth confirmed, Lorna stayed surprisingly strong. "Then you and I are not legally married."

Sighing heavily, he paused and then finally admitted, "No we're not."

Hattie and Dakota sat listening to their father, dumbfounded, grateful that their mother wasn't there to hear what he was saying. Continuing to speak to Lorna, Newton paced back and forth in front the fireplace that was beside his chair, then to the window and back. Amazingly, his whole demeanor was the essence of a perfect gentleman.

After hearing more about Minerva and his other life in Missouri, Lorna asked pointedly, "Just what do you intend to do about this situation, Newton?"

"I'll divorce Minerva and marry you in Des Moines. That way, no one around here will know. Will that make you happy?"

Before Lorna could answer, Hattie, now irate, stood and walked toward her father. "Tell me Pa, why have you made Mama and the rest of us live like paupers, when you had this kind of money?"

"I couldn't live like this with both Minerva and Lorna," he said matter-of-factly, shrugging his shoulders. "I had to make a choice. I chose Lorna."

Hearing her father's statement, resentment ran deep in Hattie's soul. Raising her voice, she was so mad she could've spit nails. "Damn you, Pa! How can you stand there and act so indifferent about things! You have no idea how hard it was for us and how hard we had to work just to scrape by." Tears formed in her eyes as she thought back to all the hard times, and how little Newton was there to help. Shaking her head blankly, she continued, "What I really don't understand, though, Pa, is why you gave the pretense of being a backwoods man in Gallatin, when all along you weren't?"

Ignoring her question, Newton again spoke to Lorna. "Lorna, I asked you if it would make you happy if I divorced Minerva and married you?"

Incensed that he was treating Hattie so rudely, Lorna said, "Answer your daughter's question, Newton! We will discuss us later."

Turning, Newton glared into Hattie's puzzled face. "You listen to me, young Lady; I'm not answerable to you, Dakota Jayne, or anyone else for that matter, so get that through your thick head!"

Stepping behind Hattie, Matthew placed his hand on her shoulder and asked quietly, "What can Cameron and I do, Miss Hattie?"

Turning her head and looking up and over her shoulder at him, she winked. She was not about to let her father get the best of her. Turning again to look Newton but still speaking to Matthew, she said, "You're a religious man, Matthew. Tell me, is there a penalty in the hereafter for killing your own father?"

Following her cue, he replied smoothly, "I suppose it depends on what he's done. In your case, I'm not sure. I would imagine there are a lot of people who would like to kill your father. In fact, I'll bet most wouldn't blame you for killing him. Rather, I think they'd commend you."

Not amused in the least by their sarcasm, Newton rose up to attack Matthew but stopped when he saw Hattie reach inside the slits of her skirt, pull out both revolvers, and aim them directly at him. Whatever happened next, it was obvious she wasn't going to let him get away with anything this time.

"You make me so mad, Pa, I could just blow your legs out from under you!"

Seeing the seriousness in her eyes, he knew the time for games was over. Speaking bluntly, he asked, "Why are you here, Hattie?"

"I'm here for one reason and one reason only, Pa. I want to know who killed Nick Starr?"

Standing motionless, he said nothing.

"Come on, Pa," Hattie said agitated, "I know you've been secretly meeting with Jess and Abner. I also know that you met with Laville before Nick's murder. Now, it's plain to see by all these secret meetings that you must know something, and as God as my witness, I'm not leaving until I find out what."

Still, he refused.

Fed up with his uncooperative attitude, Hattie pulled the triggers on both revolvers several times. The bullets screamed through the air, striking the floor right next to his feet, causing Lorna to let out a shriek of terror.

Newton, startled, leaped back in shock. Knowing he had gone too far, he opened his mouth to speak, but before he could utter a word, two more bullets whizzed past his ears and lodged in the wall behind him.

"All right! All right!" he yelled, throwing his hands up. "Damn it, Hattie, don't get your dander up!"

"I'll quit getting my dander up when you start giving me some answers," she responded angrily.

Weak-kneed, he walked back to his chair by the window and sat down with a thud. Once composed, he said, "All right, I'll answer your damn questions. I didn't spend much of my money on Minerva and you, because none of you were used to the finer things. As far as I could tell, Minerva was happy the way she was. It was different with Lorna. She came from a well-to-do family and was the widow of a man who had left her a sizeable estate. I've been a good husband to her and a good father to our children. I would think you'd appreciate that fact."

Hattie couldn't believe what he was saying. "How in the name of God could he think he could ever justify himself to me?" she thought. Shaking her head, she replied angrily, "How can you say 'as far as you could tell' Mama was happy! You were never there. And when you were, you made our lives a living hell! As for deciding which family had to live like paupers, I want to know where you got the money to live like this? Because it sure didn't come out of our little farm in Missouri."

Looking past her, he gazed blankly at the wall. Finally, after several moments, he replied straight-faced, "I'm a gambler, Hattie. Not some fly-by-night either; I'm a professional. I don't just gamble on the Mississippi River but all over the country. I gamble with the big boys where the stakes are high, and I win." Pausing, a smug smile crossed his face. "Then, I take my winnings and invest the money. I'm pleased to say, Hattie, that I'm a self-made man. I may not have the kind of money Rebecca gave you by any stretch of the imagination, but as you can see, I've done well."

"How long have you been doing this?" Dakota asked amazed.

"I started gambling long before Hattie was born, and when I wasn't doing that, I divided my time between Minerva and Lorna."

"What about Lucille Devereaux, Pa?" Hattie asked curiously.

"That's another story, Hattie, which I don't intend to discuss with you."

Trying to understand all that had happened since Hattie arrived, Lorna felt overwhelmed. "Just what is your real name, Newton?"

"It isn't important, Lorna. Knowing my real name won't change a thing."

Looking forlorn, she said, "Then Newton Anthony is not your real name?"

"No."

"Is Newton Anthony Morran your real name, Pa?" Dakota asked curiously.

"No, Cody, it isn't."

Everyone in the room was aghast. Just who was this man?

Totally disgusted, Lorna could only shake her head. Throughout this whole nightmarish ordeal, she had valiantly held on to the hope that despite of Newton's past sins they could work things out, but now, as she realized what a truly devious man Newton was, she knew that there was no chance for reconciliation. Speaking firmly, she walked toward him. "Newton, or whoever you are, I suggest that you go upstairs, pack your things, and get out. And, if you're smart, you'll never show your face here in this town again, because I intend to sign a warrant for your arrest for bigamy."

"You'd never embarrass yourself like that," he responded arrogantly.

"Oh, wouldn't I? Evidently you don't know me any better than

I know you."

Interrupting, Dakota pleaded, "Please, Pa, tell us yes or no. Do you know who killed Nick Starr?"

"Yes."

Clutching at her heart, Hattie took a ragged breath. "You nearly ruined my life once, Pa, when you forced me into marrying Abner. Why would you do it again by implicating Ira for Nick's murder, if you know it wasn't him." Raising her voice, she glared at him. "For once in your life, tell us the truth! What part did you, Abner, Jess, and Laville play in all this mess?"   Smiling smugly, Newton took on an appearance of extreme arrogance. "As you recall, Hattie, Laville was acquitted. As for the Garlands and I, we just happened to be riding in the vicinity when the whole sordid affair occurred. I know who did it, but I'll never tell. I've hated the Saxons for a long, long time, and the boy is no different. I'll be damn glad when they string him up!"

Listening to Newton, Matthew could hardly believe that he could have possibly fathered Minerva's children. They, with the exception of Laville, were all loving, caring individuals who would do anything to help someone in need.

Near her wits end, Hattie pleaded with her father. "Please put your personal feelings aside and help me save Ira. Tell me, Pa, who did it?"

"Why?"

"Because I have to know," Hattie begged.

"And then what," he stated coldly. "You would save Ira, but you would lose so much more." Glancing at Dakota then back at Hattie, he continued. "The truth is, Hattie, you can't handle the truth. Besides," he said solemnly, "it would only make things worse."

As Newton turned to walk away, Lorna put her personal anger aside and went to him. Taking his arm, she entreated him one last time to answer Hattie. "Newton, I've always known you to be a kind man. Please show some compassion for your daughter and answer her!"

Shaking his arm free, he didn't respond.

"I don't understand why you're always so dead set on hurting us, Pa," Dakota said angrily.

"Dakota and I have always tried to be good, Pa," Hattie said sincerely. "Neither of us has ever done anything to embarrass you. Why do you hate us so much?"

Tiring of the conflict, Newton walked toward the door to the parlor. Turning, his eyes were full of resentment. "You're too much like Minerva, Hattie, always whining and jumping to conclusions. And you, Dakota, are no better. Tell me, why do you feel it necessary to follow Hattie around like some pathetic pup, always ready to believe anything she tells you? If you ask me, I think you're both too damn emotional."

His efforts to discredit them in Lorna's eyes hadn't worked, and speaking boldly, she said, "Stop it, Newton, just stop it! I believe every word these girls have said, and I'll not let you treat them badly any longer. Go upstairs and pack your things. I'll not live in the same house as someone who is so tyrannical."

Without saying a word, Newton scoffed at her and stormed upstairs.

Turning to Hattie, Lorna's voice was soft and full of compassion. "I'd like for the four of you to stay with me after your father leaves. Maybe we can come to the truth, as it's obvious that Newton won't give you the answers you're seeking."

"We gratefully accept," Hattie responded gratefully. "We just need to grab our things from the hotel in town, but I must tell you, Lorna, that I also have men out by the main road. May they stay as well?"

"Men?"

"Yes, you see, I am quite wealthy," Hattie said as modestly as possible. "Because of that wealth, there have been several attempts on my life, and they are my bodyguards. I go nowhere without them."

Having a better understanding, Lorna said, "Oh yes, Dear, of course. I'll do whatever it takes to make them as comfortable as can be."

During the minutes Newton was upstairs, Hattie and Lorna conversed freely, shedding tears and finding they had many things in common, but before they could get into any great detail, Newton again stood in the doorway of the parlor.

Hattie did her best to be civil, but inside she was still very angry. "I think it would be in your best interest, Pa, if you returned to Gallatin and saw James at his office. Mama has had divorce papers waiting there for you to sign for some time now."

Looking at her, his face void of expression. "I'll do as I damn well please, Hattie." Turning to leave, he paused for a moment, turned around one last time, and speaking to her, said, "I'll see you at Ira's hanging, and believe me, I can hardly wait to see him get what's coming to him."

"Say what you want, Pa. I'll not let you destroy my dreams."

"You and your damn dreams. You always were too much of a dreamer, Hattie. When are you ever going to learn? Dreams never come true."

Interrupting, Dakota said angrily, "They damn sure don't if you're involved, Pa."

Ignoring her completely, he walked slowly to Lorna. Narrowing his eyes, he said, "This is your last chance, Lorna. I believe that we can still have something together, but if you find it necessary that we part ways, the only thing I can say to you is that you'll regret it."

"The only thing I regret," Lorna replied angrily, "is getting involved with a man like you."

Nodding, Newton said, "All right, Lorna. If that's the way you want it, that's just fine. Just remember that I gave you another chance, so don't come crying to me if things get tough." With that, he turned and quickly exited the house. Mounting his horse, he rode away in full gallop.

Taking her handkerchief, Lorna tried in vain to dry the tears in her eyes. Turning to Matthew, she said sadly, "How could I have been such a fool?"

"Don't be so hard on yourself, Ma'am. It seems that everyone who has ever known Newton has been fooled."

Before Lorna's children arrived home from school that day, Lorna came to the conclusion that Newton was far more evil than anyone had ever suspected, and even though she was frustrated and disillusioned, a bond of love quickly formed between Lorna, the girls, Matthew and Cameron.

When the children arrived later that day, Lorna took them directly to the parlor. Placing her arm around her son, she said to Hattie and Dakota with great pride, "Girls, this is your brother, Newton, Jr. He's eleven and a wonderful boy, much like my father, Israel Parker." Reaching out, Hattie took his hand and pulled him to her and embraced him. The older of the two little girls didn't wait for an introduction. Excitedly, she said, "I'm Opal. I'm nine. And this is my little sister, Helen. She's seven." Hearing their darling voices, Dakota knelt before them and opened her arms to embrace them.

Without hesitation, they went to her.

"Cody," Hattie said, "you're not going to believe this. These kids all have red hair just like mine."

Smiling, Lorna nodded her head. "That was the first thing I noticed, too."

Having everyone sit down, Lorna carefully explained to the children that Hattie and Dakota had come there to find Newton, as he was their father also. Hattie then introduced Matthew and Cameron and the other men, explaining that they were her bodyguards. The children, naturally curious, had many questions for their mother, and although it hurt, she told them lovingly the things she had learned that day about their father. Both Hattie and Dakota, who really had a way with children, won their hearts with little effort. When they were told that Dakota was blind, they couldn't believe it, as she didn't appear as though she were blind.

As the day wore on, the children were even more fascinated that Hattie was a sharpshooter, and young Newton could hardly wait for Cameron and Matthew to go up against her in a shooting match. Excitedly, they all went to the porch, as Lorna went for a looking glass for Hattie.

Just above a whisper, Matthew and Cameron jokingly asked Hattie if she wanted them to let her win, knowing full well they couldn't outshoot her even if they wanted to, and the match began.

Shooting target after target, Matthew and Cameron proved themselves to be very good, but when Hattie took the looking glass, turned around, and still hit every target they had set up even with her back to them, they conceded. The fact that their new older sister was such a crack-shot excited the children far more than learning that she was one of the wealthiest women in the country.

The following morning, Hattie and Dakota laid in bed talking for nearly an hour, trying to come to some rational conclusions for their father's behavior. Then, talking to Lorna with Matthew after getting ready for the day, Hattie was not surprised to find that Lorna remembered two men, who fit the description of Jess and Abner perfectly, coming to the house to meet with Newton often. Their names were never given, and Lorna recalled an eerie secrecy about their visits. At the time she passed it off as nothing, but now, as she reflected on the mess her life had turned into, she wished she had asked more questions.

Looking at Matthew at breakfast, Lorna asked, "Where did I go wrong?"

"Well," Matthew replied compassionately, "The one thing I've learned in life is that 'where there's smoke there's fire'. Most people don't notice it until consumes their home, but in reality, what ends up as an inferno always starts out as a spark. The key is to be wise enough to prevent the sparks or observant enough to notice the smoldering flame before it gets out of control."

After breakfast, with the promise of returning to visit again soon, they left Lorna and the children standing on the front porch with far more questions than answers. The one thing Hattie and Dakota were sure of was that Newton was involved with the Garlands, and Laville was far more guilty than anyone suspected. Beyond that, the trip had only managed to confuse Hattie even more than she had been.

Upon Hattie and Dakota's return to Gallatin, James informed

them Newton had not arrived nor had his office been contacted. Minerva was crushed when she heard of Newton's dual life, and lying in bed that night, she wondered just how much more there was that she didn't know about the man she had married. Closing her eyes, the thoughts that ran through her mind scared her, and secretly, she hoped she'd never find out.

Chapter 10
FADED LOVE

EIGHTEEN HUNDRED NINETY NINE was passing far too quickly for Hattie. The summer, which had been unusually hot and muggy, was now only a memory, and the date Judge Stepp had set for James to present his findings was quickly approaching. With only two months to go, Hattie's hope of finding evidence that could clear Ira's name was fading fast.

Late one afternoon on a beautiful September day not long after Hattie's nineteenth birthday, Shannon went looking for her. Finding her in the back court area practicing her marksmanship, he reached down, picked up four stones, and throwing them into the air, he said with a smile, "Hit these."

Glancing over her shoulder at her elder brother, Hattie watched as he threw the rocks out into the open sky, and then, with perfect accuracy, she hit each one of them before they struck the ground.

Thoroughly amazed, Shannon joked, "I think that's quite enough shooting for today, Sis. As I see it, you'll never get any better. You never miss."

"Now Shannon," Hattie said firmly, "you know darn well that I don't practice to become better; I practice so that I won't lose the talent God has given me. You know how the old saying goes when it comes to talent, 'either use it or lose it', and I, for one, am not about to let that happen to me."

Taking her hand gently, Shannon could only nod his head. Her wisdom never ceased to amaze him, and after taking a deep breath of the fresh autumn air, he said, "All right little Miss Annie Oakley, you're right, but why don't you put your gun away for now and go for a walk with me." Leading her toward the edge of the court area, he continued, "It's been far too long since we've had any time alone, and I have a couple of things I need to talk to you about."

So, after putting her revolvers back in her holsters through the slits in her dress, Hattie walked hand in hand with Shannon through the gardens toward the gazebo followed by Matthew and a number of her men. After walking several yards, Hattie looked up at her brother and said politely, "Before we get to what you want to talk about, Shannon, would you mind if I ask you a couple questions of my own."

"Sure, shoot."

"Tell me; is Robert really happy down in Caldwell County, now that he's married to Amanda Brown?"

"Yes, he is. In fact when I was down there the other day, he told me how thankful he was for everything you have done for him."

"Oh, Shannon, that's wonderful," Hattie responded with a smile. "I worry about him and John so much. I hate that I don't get to see them as often as I'd like, but if they're happy, that's all that matters." Taking a deep breath, she paused momentarily then asked the question that was really weighing on her mind. "Do you know of anyone who would want to move into the little farm house Ira and I bought? I'd like to have someone out there to watch the place."

"Do you want to sell it?"

"No, not really. I was approached by a couple last week who

wanted to buy it, but I know that one day, it's going to be one of the only memories of Ira that I will have left." Stopping in front of the gazebo, she glanced heavenward. "You know, Shannon, in spite of everything that has happened, I can't help but believe that Ira is going to hang for something he didn't do." Turning away, she sighed wearily. "Why Ira and Pa are trying to protect whoever really did kill Nick, I'll never know." Then, looking up at him again, Hattie said, "I'm sorry, Shannon, I'm rambling. What was it that you wanted to talk to me about?"

"Well, I have good news and bad news, but believe it or not, they both have to do with Pa."

"You're right," Hattie replied sarcastically, "I don't believe it. After all that he has put Lorna through the past two months, I have a hard time believing that anything connected with him could be good news."

"Most of it isn't," Shannon responded solemnly.

Walking over to the gazebo, Hattie leaned her back up against it. The mere thought of more bad news involving her Pa made her sick. After taking several deep breaths to calm herself, she spoke softly to her brother. "Okay, Shannon, give me the bad news first. At least that way I know that I'll have something good to look forward to."

"First of all, you remember how Pa has been harassing Lorna the past six weeks to move out of their home in Keokuk?"

"How could I forget? Lorna has been worrying herself sick about it. So, after one of her last telegrams, James hired three gunmen to go up there and stay with her and the kids."

"Well, apparently the county judge up there is one of Pa's best friends, and even though Pa is a proven bigamist, the judge sent a deputy out to Lorna with a court order informing her that she has one week to move out. The court order said that because Lorna was never legally married to Pa, she has no legal rights to his property, house, or money. She telegrammed James today with the news while I was at his office in town. Needless to say, she is pretty shook up about the whole thing, and she doesn't know what to do."

Hearing the news, Hattie could only shake her head in disgust. "Just when I think Pa can't get any lower or can't possibly hurt anybody anymore than he has, he goes out and proves me wrong." Pacing back and forth in front of the gazebo, her jaw was firmly set and her eyes were aflame with anger.

Walking to Hattie's side, Shannon placed his hands on her shoulders, stopping her from moving. His gentle touch always had a way of calming her, and as she looked up and into his loving eyes, her demeanor instantly softened.

"So, what's the good news?" Hattie asked with a sigh.

Reaching into his coat pocket, Shannon pulled out some papers, and handing them to Hattie, he said, "Look for yourself."

Glancing over the papers, Hattie couldn't believe her eyes, as there, right in her own hands, were the divorce papers James had drawn up for her mother from Newton, and they were signed. "When did he do this?" Hattie asked anxiously.

"Sometime yesterday, I guess. James had left them with his secretary for what seemed like forever, but when he arrived at work this morning, they were signed."

Dumbfounded, Hattie could only muster one word. "Amazing." Then, realizing what this meant, her heart leaped. "Oh, Shannon," she said excitedly, "Mama is going to be so relieved!"

"Boy, you ain't kidding, Sis. Mama has nearly worried herself sick ever since you and Dakota returned from Keokuk. Hearing about Pa's other life really rattled her. She told me several times in the last month that she desperately wanted those papers signed so that she could finally put that part of her life behind her. And by the grace of God, it appears she got her wish."

Moving into the gazebo, Hattie sat down, still quite dazed by the sudden turn of events. Closing her eyes for a minute, Hattie tried to quiet her mind, but try as she did to relax, she couldn't help but think about Lorna and her unfortunate set of circumstances. Looking at Shannon, who was now sitting across from her, she knew that somehow they must help her. Sitting silently, an idea began to formulate in her mind, and it was becoming perfectly clear to her exactly what needed to be done.

As if he was reading her mind, Shannon said, "So, Sister Dear, what are you going to do for Lorna Anthony?"

Taken aback by her brother's perception, Hattie replied, "Why, whatever do you mean?"

"You know exactly what I mean," Shannon shot back without hesitation. "You've never been the one to turn your back on someone in need, and I doubt you are going to start with Lorna." Smiling slyly, he had her pegged, and he knew it. "So, fess up, Sis, what's going on in that big heart of yours."

"Boy," Hattie said candidly, "you don't miss a trick, do you, Shannon?"

"Not when it comes to you, Hattie. I've known you too long."

"Well if you must know, the first thing I'm going to do is set up one of my Chicago companies so that all of the profits go into a bank account for Lorna and the children. Then, the second thing I'm going to do is have Mama write a letter to Lorna inviting her to stay with us for a while. I figure if the letter comes from Mama, she will feel more comfortable about the whole deal. Besides, Mama has wanted to meet Lorna and her children ever since she found out about them. She feels like they should be friends, and I agree wholeheartedly. Just don't go spilling the beans to anyone. I want this to be a surprise."

"Mum's the word." Getting to his feet, Shannon couldn't help but smile at Hattie's generosity. He knew she'd come through; she always did. "Come," Shannon urged, "let's go sit by the creek, it's a little quieter down there, and I've got one more thing I want you to take a look at."

Intrigued, Hattie followed him quietly, and upon reaching the creek, he handed her a letter from Rebecca. Reading it, Hattie's face took on a solemn look. "Gee," Hattie said, breaking the silence. "That is certainly interesting. Why did she send this to you?"

"You know as well I do that it is getting harder to trust folks these days, and my guess is that she was afraid if she mailed it to you, someone at the post office would intercept it. You can just bet that Pa, Jess, Abner, and even Laville have got people all over doing their dirty work." Pausing, Shannon picked up a stone and skipped it across the creek. "I don't know what I'm going to do about the terrible way I feel about Laville. She makes me so damn mad I can't even think straight!" Looking at Hattie with genuine concern, he added, "I'll bet I end up burning in hell just for the way I feel about her."

"Bull Feathers! You're the last person in this world who will ever end up burning in hell for anything. You're one of the most loving people I have ever known, and I'm sure the Almighty has a special place in heaven for you."

Sitting down on a boulder, Shannon entrenched himself in

silence. After several minutes, he finally looked up at Hattie, who had taken a minute to admire the beginning of the beautiful autumn colors on the trees by the creek, and asked, "What do you plan to do when this is all over?"

Not knowing exactly what he meant, she walked toward him and sat on a nearby boulder. "You mean Ira's hanging?"

"Yes."

"Well, given the new information in this letter from Rebecca, my plans are definitely going to be different. I was expecting her and Lou to be home soon, but seeing as how they have been receiving death threats and will be staying in Richmond, I will probably go there to visit them. I have been thinking about taking Katherine and traveling for some time, and the last place I'm going to want to be after such a horrible event is here. There will just be too many memories. Getting out and seeing a little of the world will probably do me good. Besides, with James and Dakota living here at the estate, I know that things will be taken care of perfectly." Pausing, Hattie looked over at Shannon, and the look of concern on his face worried her. "What is it, Shannon? Was it something I said?"

Turning to face her, he sighed heavily. "You know, I've not said much about Ira's trial, but something is terribly wrong, and I can't seem to put my finger on it. For Ira to be convicted of killing Nick over money has got to be a lie to cover up the real reason he was killed. That one fact, more than any other about the whole trial, just doesn't add up in my mind." Taking a deep breath, he continued, "If you ask me, it seems like Ira is covering up something. What do you think?"

"Absolutely," Hattie answered with great conviction. "I have felt that way ever since the day the Sheriff came to Silver Creek to arrest him. He knew more than he led onto then, and after watching him throughout the trial, I now have no doubt that he knows exactly who killed Nick. But for reasons that I cannot understand, he will not tell anyone what he knows. His eerie silence about the events of that night is the very reason that James and I hired so many private investigators. After the Judge agreed to postpone the hanging, James was able to send people all over the country to try and dig up information. Jacob Jones was the one that informed us about Pa's duel life in Keokuk, but we also had several investigators checking into Nick's past as well. They confirmed what Ira had told me about Nick's being married once before in Wichita, and they also confirmed what he said about her being mysteriously murdered."

"Really?"

"Just wait, it gets more interesting. What Ira didn't tell me, and the investigators did, is that it happened while Nick's eighteen-year-old nephew, Philip Langley, was living with them. Supposedly, he and Nick were out of town the night of the murder. Their alibis held up so, of course, neither of them were charged, but Nick definitely didn't hurt by her death financially, as she was quite wealthy. Before her death, Nick had been just an average guy, but her death left him with a sizeable fortune."

"Interesting," Shannon said, as he listened intently.

"There's still more," Hattie replied candidly. "A few months after the funeral, there was a falling out between Nick and his nephew, Phillip. The young man left town infuriated, threatening to get even with Nick if it was the last thing he ever did, but no one has ever seen or heard of him again."

"Strange."

"Yeah, well, even stranger is a few months later, Nick sold

everything in Wichita and moved to Kansas City. At that same time, Ira was staying and working with his uncle, Peter Saxon. Peter also lived in Kansas City, and quite coincidently, was an old schoolmate of Nicks. When Nick came into town that October, he looked up Peter and subsequently met Ira."

"So why don't you have someone talk to Peter, Sis? He must know a lot about Nick, being his schoolmate and all."

"We tried, but unfortunately, Peter died about six months ago only weeks after Andrew, and his wife has since moved back to the east coast."

Sighing heavily, Shannon looked toward the clearing leading to the mansion and was surprised to see James and Dakota walking together toward them.

Rising to his feet, he called out to them. "James! Dakota! Over here!"

"There you two are," James said, getting closer. "Minerva was worried that you two had fallen off the face of the earth, so she sent us out to find you."

Inviting them to sit with them by the creek, Hattie said, "I was in the middle of telling Shannon about the things we found out about Nick through the investigators."

"Really," James replied with interest, as he sat down on a boulder. "How far did you get?"

"Right up to the point where Ira and Nick met, but I'm afraid I'm a bit sketchy about what happened next. Would you mind continuing from that point, James?"

"Sure." Turning to Shannon, James began. "The day they met, Nick had already planned a huge dinner party for that night, celebrating his arrival to Kansas City. It was October, 1st 1896, a little over two months after Hattie's wedding to Abner. With all the new wealth Nick had inherited from his wife's death, he commanded respect, and with hopes of further enhancing his social and business status, he invited all of the city's most important citizens to the party. Having known Peter from way back and taking a liking to Ira, he invited them to the party. Ira, even though he was nineteen at the time, was still young and impressionable, and he was immediately taken with Nick confidence, style, and wealth."

"So what happened at the party?" Shannon asked anxiously.

"Well, poor Ira was in over his head from the beginning. First, he arrived in clothes that were too small for him, looking like a backwoods hick, which, up to that point, is what he was. Then, to make matters worse, he had no knowledge of proper etiquette or style. He was truly a fish out of water, but the sight of all the gorgeous women that Nick had on his arm that evening coupled with his great wealth and style apparently enticed Ira enough to want to get know him better. He went over to Nick's house frequently in the days following the party, and after only a couple weeks, Nick invited Ira, a total stranger before that point, to come live with him."

Politely interrupting, Shannon said, "Hold, on a minute, James. How could that have happened without anyone knowing? Did Ira ever write anything to you through Emily about Nick, Hattie?"

"No, he didn't, Shannon," Hattie replied matter-of-factly. "That is something that bothered me from the moment I found out that Nick and Ira were friends, and I asked James to ask the investigators about that very thing."

Turning back to James, Shannon asked, "And what did they say?"

"Apparently, Ira's work with his uncle finished much earlier than he let on to Hattie in his letters, allowing him the freedom to move in with Nick. Now, where it gets crazy is that even though Peter and his wife knew what Ira was doing, the rest of Ira's family and Hattie had no idea."

"How is that possible?" Dakota asked, bewildered. "I know well enough from talking with Emily that even though the two families didn't visit each other very often because of Andrew and Peter's failing health, they kept in contact regularly by mail."

"The investigators believe that Nick had a friend at the post office, and he intercepted all mail going between Peter and Ira's family, enabling Nick and Ira to keep everyone in the dark about the truth."

"Unbelievable!" Shannon replied in amazement.

"Just wait, it gets even crazier. Six months after Ira moved in with Nick, there was another formal dinner held at Nick's home, and lo and behold, this time Ira was by his side looking like a million dollars and presenting himself like a well-bred gentleman. It was said that every available woman with money was invited that evening, and Ira was surrounded by them. As Nick had been with his nephew, Phillip Langley, he and Ira became inseparable. They appeared at every social gathering the rest of that summer in Kansas City as well as the Capitol, always with the richest and most beautiful women on their arms."

"But, James," Shannon interjected again, "Ira courted and married Hattie."

Speaking before James could respond, Dakota said, "Now, Shannon, let's be totally honest about this. Even though Ira and Hattie had agreed to wait for each other, we all know that it was Hattie who chased after Ira, not the other way around."

Rolling her eyes, Hattie let out a ragged breath. "You're right, Cody, I did."

"Regardless of who went after who," James continued, "Nick felt that he had a prize stallion in Ira. There's little doubt to me now that it was his intention all along to marry Ira off to the woman with the most money, or in other words, Nick wanted to sell him off to the highest bidder."

Disgusted, Dakota's voice was full of anger. "You have got to be kidding me!"

"I wish I was," James replied solemnly. "Unfortunately, all the evidence the investigators gathered points to this fact. Remember our first meeting with Nick on the train on our way home from Chicago, Hattie? What would you like to bet that it wasn't by mere chance? He undoubtedly already knew of your immense fortune and planned in some way for Ira to get it." Pausing, James made his way to Hattie. "Remember how ill you were until Ira's arrest? I hate to say it, Hattie, but I believe that Ira was slowly poisoning you."

Wearily, Hattie looked into the faces of those around her. "Could that be the motive behind Ira's having killed Nick? I don't think that Ira wanted to kill me, so killing Nick or having him killed would have been Ira's only option to be free of Nick's control, wouldn't it?"

Nodding affirmatively, James looked at Hattie with great compassion. "Sad as it is, that has become my consensus, Hattie. I've had suspicions of it ever since Matthew told me about a conversation that he had with Doc Cowley shortly after Ira's incarceration. The good doctor found a vial of poison on Nick the night of the murder whose symptoms, when applied to humans in small doses, matched the ones you were experiencing. I didn't tell you tell at first, Hattie, because I wanted to have more proof. Now, however, with the investigators' findings in hand, it is clearer to me more than ever that

Ira and Nick were working together in some way to get your fortune. In fact, it is quite obvious to me now that Nick had privately educated and trained Ira for one purpose and one purpose alone, to marry and then plunder rich women."

"Unbelievable," Dakota said, still not able to believe what she was hearing.

"The only problem, it seems, is that near the completion of Nick's plan, I believe that Ira refused to cooperate, which led to the great tension between them that we all observed, fierce arguments, and eventually Nick's death."

"James, are you absolutely sure about all this," Shannon asked hesitantly. "We're talking about cold-blooded murder here. Do you honestly think that it came to that for Ira?"

"People do strange things when under great stress, Shannon," James replied candidly. "Things they would never think about doing normally all of a sudden don't look so bad when their backs are against the wall."

Nodding his head, Shannon conceded. "Okay, so say it was Ira. What I still don't get is why Ira hung around Nick in the first place. Nick was old enough to be his father. Why did feel that he needed a father-figure when he already had a wonderful father in Andrew?"

"I wondered the same thing, Shannon. When I was visiting him several weeks ago, I asked Ira about his unusual relationship with Nick, and he became very angry and defensive. Then, when I pushed the issue and asked if his relationship was the same type as the one that Phillip Langley had had with Nick, Ira became so upset that he refused to talk with me anymore, and he had me escorted out of the jail. At the time, I didn't know exactly what it all meant, but the more information that came in from the investigators, the more the pieces of this puzzle began to come together."

"Wait a minute here," Hattie interjected bewildered, "just what kind of relationship are we talking about, James?"

Taking a deep breath, James chose his words very carefully. "Above all, let's not any of us be judgmental, but the relationship I am talking about is one between lovers."

Instinctively reaching out for Hattie's hand to offer support, Dakota spoke softly. "Oh, Hattie, as much as I hate to think about it, somehow I feel what James is saying is true."

Still in shock, Hattie's mind raced back to all of Ira's early morning rides with Nick that lasted for hours and also back to all of the late night meetings he had with Nick at the mill. All of sudden, it made perfect sense. Staring ahead blankly, Hattie said in a weak voice, "Oh, God, I think you're right, James. Looking back at Ira's behavior throughout our relationship, it is obvious that there was much more going on between Ira and Nick then any of us could have ever imagined."

Sitting in complete silence, everyone took a moment to digest this new revelation concerning Nick and Ira. Finally, after what seemed like an eternity, Dakota turned to James and said, "Everything else aside, what seems strange to me is Nick supposedly signing that ridiculous death statement with an X. Despicable or not, I can't conceive anyone as well-educated as Nick signing something so important with an X. It certainly doesn't hold true to Nick's meticulous nature. I mean, Nick Starr isn't a very long name. You'd think he could have at least made an attempt to scribble it, don't you think? I don't know about the rest of you, but if I was naming my murderer, I certainly wouldn't sign my name with an X. Oh, and the fact that Laville was the one who wrote the death statement," she added emphatically, "is highly suspicious. It wouldn't surprise me one bit if she didn't forge the statement to take the heat off of herself for her involvement, which, sad to say, I feel is greater than anyone knows." Crossing her arms angrily, it was obvious that this was a touchy issue to Dakota.

Reaching over to calm her, Shannon said, "I agree with you one hundred percent, Sis. It simply amazes me that the jury accepted that statement as evidence. Its things like that about the trial that make me believe, without a doubt, that it was rigged. And then, to top off all of the craziness, Ira refused to cooperate to save his own life."

Sitting quiet, Hattie desperately tried to go over every minute of every day that she had spent with Ira since the beginning of their engagement. Nothing about her life seemed to make sense anymore, and the more she thought about things, the more disillusioned she became. Then, just as she thought she had reached her wits end, Hattie felt the presence of someone behind her. Instinctively, she knew it was Matthew, and upon turning around, she could see him hiding in a grove of trees near her. Calling to him, she said, "For heaven's sake, Matthew, will you and the other men please come over here and stop lurking around in the trees like a bunch of thieves. Given how uneasy I feel right now, I want you fellas closer to me than a stamp on a letter."

Laughing slightly, Matthew and the other men quickly fell in around the family. "We were just trying to give you ample privacy, Hattie, but if you want us, we're here."

Chuckling to herself for a moment, Dakota's mood soon turned serious again, as she said, "You know, Matthew, I want to tell you something. I haven't worried one minute about Hattie since James hired you to watch over her. Believe me, you have no idea how much we appreciate you and the men."

"Thank you very much, Dakota," Matthew replied graciously. "It's always nice to be appreciated." Then, moving in directly behind Hattie, Matthew stood over her. "Like I said before, we didn't want to interrupt your time alone with Shannon, and when James and Dakota showed up, we thought it would be best if we stay in the background. Are we making you nervous, Hattie?"

"You, heavens no, but I do feel like I'm about to go crazy. There are so many unanswered questions about this situation with Ira that it seems like hardly anything makes sense anymore. Like James found out, just let any of us approach him or probe too much for information and he becomes extremely defensive. It is pretty obvious to all of us that he is hiding something, trying to protect someone, or both."

"If he is protecting someone, it would have to be someone he really cares about," Matthew said emphatically.

Just then, Dakota had a fleeting memory. Closing her eyes tightly, a picture began to form in her mind. Through a fog, she saw several people standing along a roadside arguing, followed by the shriek of a woman in the distance, and lastly a gunshot, but to Dakota's bewilderment, just as quickly as the picture had appeared, it was gone. Shaking her head, she thought she was going crazy.

Noticing Dakota's uneasiness, Hattie touched her hand, but after Dakota reassured her that she would be okay, Hattie looked heavenward and sighed heavily. "Even with help from all of you, I don't know how in the world I'm going to get through the next few months. We have just got to find something that can clear Ira, because, to be honest with all of you, I don't know if I can deal with the hanging. There have been all sorts of awful rumors and threats, everything from people building stockades around the gallows and charging money to threats over what is going to happen to Ira's body afterward. And according to a letter Shannon got today, even Rebecca and Lou have been harassed. I just don't know how much more I can handle." Leaning back into Matthew's strong arms, Hattie again felt like she was near her wits end.

Holding Hattie in his arms for a moment, Matthew moved around to face her. "If you're that worried about what might happen to Ira's body, then we need to be making plans to protect him now."

"I do have an idea, Matthew," she replied, rising to her feet. "But I'll need all of the family and the Sheriff to help me if it's going to work."

Anxious to help in any way possible, Shannon encouraged Hattie to tell them what she had in mind. After hearing her out, he was very supportive. "Sounds good to me, Sis. How about everyone else?" Looking around, everyone was in total agreement. "Great, it's settled then, and Hattie, if you ask me, this really is the best choice."

"I sure hope so, because I don't want Ira's body disgraced in any way. Even if he hasn't been the perfect husband, I care about him too much to let something like that happen."

Seeing she needed support, Matthew took Hattie in his arms and embraced her tenderly. She was shaking like a leaf, but throughout everything, she somehow managed to hold things together. "You've grown to love Ira a great deal, haven't you, Hattie?" he asked politely.

"Love Ira? I'm not sure about that anymore," she replied honestly. "I really thought I loved him in the months after we found him in North Dakota. He seemed to have all the right answers, yet even then, something was never quite right. Then, two days after we were married, he turned cold, and it wasn't long afterward that he was arrested. With the way our life together ended up, and with so little time as husband and wife, it was impossible to develop any real deep feelings for him. After his arrest, our relationship as husband and wife ended, and whatever feelings I once had are now little more than 'faded love'. It took me a long time to accept the fact that all the hopes and dreams I had of spending my life with him, bearing his children, and our growing old together, just weren't going to happen. And now as I look back, it seems that even the few days that we did have together had a dark cloud hanging over them. It's sad to say, but Nick's death and Ira's involvement, whatever it was, has cheated me out of my dreams."

"Just remember," James reminded her, "that we don't know exactly what happened that night. Despite our best efforts to ascertain the truth, only God knows what happened. I could be completely off the mark with my theories, but until Ira opens up to one of us, we'll never know."

"Don't lose hope, Hattie," Matthew encouraged. "We never know what will happen from one day to the next, but remember you can be assured that there is a day of reckoning. Every man and woman will have to stand before God and give an accounting of what they've done."

Shannon, who was now walking back in forth by the creek, spoke solemnly. "The last time I was with Ira that was what he seemed to be most concerned about. He told me that he was sure he was going straight to Hell. I asked him if he hadn't killed Nick why he felt that way, but he didn't answer. He just shook his head, turned, and walked away."

"Well, let's get something straight right now, Shannon," Hattie stated emphatically, "Hell has never scared me. I figure when the final judgment is over, if I have to, I'll walk straight down there with both guns blazing, and I'll guarantee you that not even the devil himself will hold on to those I care about."

"You got that right, Sis," Dakota replied jokingly. "Not even the devil is that brave."

After everyone chuckled for a moment, Hattie looked up into Matthew's loving face, smiled, then lay her head on his massive chest. Standing motionless, Hattie could hear his heart beating rhythmically. With her arms about him, she said softly, "Matthew Stuart Forsythe, you're one of the best things that has ever happened to me. Your faith, friendship, and loyalty are so refreshing, and what you said a minute ago is the absolute truth. No matter what happens, we must not give up hope. It is one of the most important emotions that a human being can feel. Hope is what gives and maintains life, hope is what encourages us to keep going when we feel like we've taken the last step we can possibly take, and most importantly, hope is what heals us when we've been hurt. Without hope, life would cease to be bearable. Even if nothing in life is working for us, if we can somehow hold on to a flicker of hope, we can make it through the rainy days of our life to once again bask in the sunlight of happiness. So, given all that, thank you, Matthew, for being my hope during this whole sordid ordeal. Without you, I don't think I could have gotten this far, and I know that in the months ahead, I am going to need you even more."

"Gee," Matthew said behind a blushing smile. "I believe that's about the nicest thing anyone has ever said to me."

"Well, it's true," Hattie replied sincerely. "You and your brothers deserve every good thing that this world has to offer. It always amazes me when I see you together. You are all so open and loving with each other. Ira, on the other hand, always seems to be so closed off, and as hard as I've tried, I simply cannot reach him. Even if I spent a dozen lifetimes with him, I don't think I would ever know him half as well as I do you. I am truly blessed to have you in my life."

"I'm the lucky one, Hattie," Matthew responded earnestly. "I'm the lucky one."

Rising to their feet after the long conversation, Dakota and James said goodbye and slowly made their way back to the house, leaving Hattie, Shannon, and Matthew to walk east along the creek toward the main road about a mile away on the opposite side of the mansion. Because the gardeners maintained everything so well, Hattie loved walking on the grounds of Silver Creek. Following the creek was especially enjoyable for Hattie, as the sound of the running water always seemed to calm her nerves.

Followed by a number of her men, Hattie, Shannon, and Matthew reached the main road just in time to see a carriage making its way toward the mansion. As it drew near to them, Shannon called out in a booming voice, "Who's there?"

"It's me, Shannon," rang out an all too familiar voice. "It's me, Laville."

Turning back to Hattie, Shannon rolled his eyes. "Why did I have to ask?"

Bringing her carriage to an abrupt halt, Laville anxiously jumped out and made her way to them. Squealing excitedly, she called out to Matthew with a big smile on her face. "Break out the champagne, Matthew! It's time for celebration!" Then, approaching Hattie and

Shannon, Laville could hardly contain her excitement. "Boy do I have good news for both of you!" she crowed.

Dumbfounded by Laville's unexplainable euphoria, Hattie asked curiously, "What, Laville, what?"

"It's the best news this century! Our Pa is finally dead!"

Hearing the news, Shannon and Hattie stood in disbelief for what seemed like an eternity, looking first back and forth at each other, then at Matthew, and finally back at Laville. Finally gaining his wits, Shannon replied, "Great news, Laville? You call the death of our Pa great news?"

Hattie, shocked and weakened, tried in vain to control her emotions. "Are you sick, Laville?" Hattie replied in anger.

"Me, sick? I think not, Hattie. How can you call me sick, when you're the one who's married to a convicted murderer?"

Leaving Hattie's side, Matthew went to Laville. "Are you absolutely sure about this, Laville?"

"Honey, I've never been so sure nor happy about anything in all my life!" Laville cooed. "Pa's deader than a doornail. He died in Princeton last night in a hotel fire. His body was burnt pretty badly, but the law in Princeton said they were sure it was Pa. They sent Sheriff Sanders a telegram late this morning, and I just happened to bump into him at the telegram office." Holding up a yellow piece of paper, she smiled smugly. "I've even got the telegram to prove it!"

Shocked by Laville's callousness, Matthew replied, "Do you really feel that it's appropriate to speak of your father's death in such a flippant manner?"

"Listen, Matthew," Laville retorted, "I like you. I like you a lot. But don't push your luck with me on this one, Honey. I am only too happy to see that bastard get his just desserts."

Apprehensively taking the telegram from Laville's hand, Hattie studied it in silence. Reaching the end, she let out a ragged breath. Something about all this just didn't make sense to her. Giving the telegram to Shannon, Hattie looked up at Laville and said, "The telegram says that Pa's body was burnt beyond recognition, so how could anyone know if it was really him?"

"I can't believe you, Hattie," Laville answered angrily. "Leave it to you to question the law. For hell's sake, why can't you just accept the truth?"

"I'm with Hattie on this Laville," Shannon interrupted. "Nothing about this makes sense. Pa went to a lot of trouble to force Lorna out of their home in Keokuk. Then, after months of waiting, he finally shows up and signs the divorce papers from Mama, and now, suddenly, he's dead. It's too unbelievable."

"Look," Laville spouted back annoyed, "Sheriff Sanders confirmed the report to me himself. He said that the Princeton Sheriff had evidence that Pa was in the hotel. If you can't believe me, surely you believe him."

Nodding her head, Hattie's thoughts turned to Ira. Her Pa had been her last hope in finding out what really happened to Nick, but with the unexpected news of his death, her hopes of finding out the truth were fading fast. "You're right, Laville. Sheriff Sanders is a good man. If he believes that Pa is dead, he must have solid evidence."

Thrilled that Hattie was finally coming around, Laville exclaimed, "Now, like I said earlier, lets break out the champagne and celebrate!"

Angered by Laville's callous words, Hattie replied firmly, "How in the world can you be so unfeeling, Laville? I'll admit that Pa wasn't my favorite person and neither did I like the things he did, but he was our father. And I, unlike you, cannot bring myself to rejoice in his or anyone else's death."

"You didn't know Pa like I did!" Laville shot back with her eyes aflame in anger. "I hated him so much I wish he would have died years ago! All of us kids, Mama, and Lorna would have been a hell of a lot better off if he had!" Turning, she tried to calm herself and began walking toward her buggy. "Now, since none of you seem to share my joy in this, I'm going to tell Mama. Lord knows she could use some good news."

"Wait a minute, Laville!" Shannon insisted. "I think it would be better if we all told her together."

Perturbed, Laville turned around and snipped, "Oh, all right, if you want to steal my thunder then just go tell her yourselves." Continuing on to her buggy, she climbed up onto it hurriedly. Then, as if she just remembered something, she turned back toward Hattie. "By the way, Hattie, I've decided to sell the Anderson farm and Nick's big house in town."

"Okay," Hattie replied, "but what does that have to do with me?"

"I want you to buy them of course. And I want at least twice as much as anyone else would pay for them. I've got big plans, and I do not intend to stay in Gallatin for the rest of my life."

Tired of Laville's antics, Shannon started to protest, but knowing that arguing with her would do them no good, Hattie shushed him. "Tell James I said to write you a check for whatever amount you want," Hattie agreed, in an effort to keep peace.

Smiling smugly, Laville picked up the reins of her buggy and asked, "I suppose I can continue to depend on my yearly allowance from you as well?"

Looking first at Matthew and Shannon, who stood by in disbelief, and then back at Laville, Hattie responded without as much as a flinch, "Of course, Laville. No matter what happens that money will always be there for you."

Satisfied that she accomplished everything she came for, Laville gave a final yank on the reins, tossed her raven black hair over her shoulder triumphantly, and rode swiftly down the road.

Standing quietly watching her buggy speed away, Hattie, Shannon, and Matthew could not help but marvel at the creature that was Laville. "I don't understand her," Shannon stated with great discouragement. "How can anyone be so cold and heartless?"

"She definitely is a strange woman," Matthew replied, but then, with increased compassion, he said, "However, we don't know all that has happened in her life. People as defensive and unfeeling as Laville are not that way by accident. They become that way because of something that has happened in their life. Sustained abuse of any kind or one very traumatic event are the most common reasons that a person's attitude turns sour, but in reality, it can be anything that their mind can't deal with. Because they don't know how to handle the pain they are going through, they become defensive, irritable, or in Laville's case very angry and vindictive. I've only seen a couple of examples as severe as Laville's in my life, but it is obvious to me now that she has been through a lot more than any of us are aware of."

* * *

A COUPLE MILES FROM THE ESTATE, Laville began to feel a pain building up at the back of her head as she rode in her carriage. Worried that it might get worse, she quickly pulled her carriage to the side of the road. She hoped desperately that the pain would go away, but as the minutes went by and the pain intensified, Laville knew this was becoming the type of excruciating headache that occasionally left her unconscious. Trying to dull the pain, she bit down on the reins of her buggy, but it was to no avail. Within moments the pain overwhelmed her, and she fainted across the seat of the carriage.

Chapter 11
SECRETS OF THE HEART

PULLING UP IN FRONT OF THE MANSION, George was still in shock. Stopping his buggy abruptly, he climbed down and hurried to the front door. He would have run, but in his old age, his body didn't move quite as well as it used to. With his heart racing, he burst into the house and yelled for help.

Hearing him, James came running from his study to see what the matter was. "For God's sake, George, what is it?"

"It be that darn Laville, Mr. James," George stated emphatically. "I be comin' home from the mercantile store in town like Miss Hattie be a wantin', when, about two miles from the estate, I be runnin' into Laville hunched over in her buggy as lifeless as a turkey on Thanksgiving. I thought she be dead at first, but after I be lookin' closer, I be seein' that she still be breathin', so I put her in me buggy and hightailed it back here as quickly as possible. Me thinks she had one of her headaches, Mr. James, so you best be gettin' Mary and tell her to bring the smellin' salts and a wet washcloth right away."

"Okay," James replied calmly, knowing exactly what to do. "George, get one of the younger boys to help you bring Laville into the parlor, and I'll be back with Mary in a heartbeat."

Just hearing James's voice, George felt better. It never ceased to amaze him how well James could handle even the most delicate of situations with grace and dignity, and Laville's sudden illness was no different. James, like Hattie, put family above everything else in his life, and even though he didn't like a lot of the things Laville did, he was completely dedicated to her because she was part of the family. "Family," James would often say, "is the most important thing in this world next to having love for God in your heart. Work, school, and religion should all have their proper places in life," he would continue, "but none of them should hamper or threaten your place with your family. They have to come first."

Everyone arrived in the parlor at about the same time, and once George and Curtis set Laville down on the settee, Mary immediately began administering the smelling salts. Minerva tried to help by holding a wet washcloth on Laville's forehead while Dakota sat silent in a chair by the fireplace. Looking up at James, Minerva asked, "When in the name of God are Hattie, Shannon, and Matthew going to get back from their walk? It's almost dark outside, and they need to be here."

"I see 'em comin' around the front now, Ma," Curtis interrupted, as he glanced out the window.

"Good," she replied in relief. "Go outside and tell them what's happened and to get in here as soon as possible. And Curtis," she added sternly, "please pronounce your words right."

"Yes, Mama."

"I mean it. How many times have I gone over this with you and your younger brothers? I don't want you sounding like a bunch of country hicks. That type of behavior is just not acceptable anymore."

"It works for George and Mary."

"George and Mary are Irish, Curtis. They have spoken that way their entire life. It is not easy to change something that you have done your whole life. That is why I want you to concentrate on correcting your speech now, before it becomes too hard for you to change. Always remember, Son, that it is much easier to build and correct a child than it is to repair an adult." Reaching out and taking his hand lovingly, she continued, "You can also look at it from the spiritual point of view. My father always used to say, 'to whom much is given, much is expected,' and God has blessed us immensely these past few years. So, to put it plainly, when you don't do your best to correct your speech, not only are you be hurting yourself in the long run, but you are also offending God. To do something like that would be stupid, and no one has the right to be stupid. Do you understand?"

"Yes, Mama, I do."

"Good. Now, please hurry and get your brother and sister. And Curtis . . ."

"Yes."

"I love you."

"I know, Mama. I love you too."

Watching him leave, Minerva hoped that what she said had gotten through. Her mother's heart had a special place for each of her children, but even more so with Curtis because he almost died at birth. The umbilical cord connecting her to him got wrapped around his neck when he was being born, and if it hadn't been for the quick actions of Doc Cowley, he surely would have died. Now, though, at nearly fifteen, Curtis was developing into a strong young man. He was already quite tall for his age at five foot ten, and his still developing body was perfectly accented by his wavy brown hair, blue eyes, and beautiful smile. Minerva had no doubt that he would be a very handsome man, but as she knew all too well from dealing with

Laville, good looks only get you so far in life.

As Hattie, Shannon, and Matthew hurriedly entered the parlor, they were full of worry and questions. "What happened?" Hattie asked anxiously.

Walking to Hattie, George again told his story, while everyone listened in silence. Once he finished, Hattie made her way to Mary and asked, "What seems to be wrong, Mary? How is she?"

"I not be knowin', Lass. George and I be thinkin' that she be havin' one of her headaches, but if she did, it be a doozey. These smellin' salts usually be workin' right away, but today they be helpin' Miss Laville very little."

"This is crazy," Matthew said, as he paced back and forth by the fireplace. "We were just with her a little under an hour ago."

"You mean she talked to you?" Minerva asked, puzzled.

"Unfortunately," Shannon replied sarcastically. "She was her usual charming self."

"Stop it, Shannon," Minerva responded sternly. "This is no time to be joking." Turning to Hattie, Minerva turned deadly serious. "What did she talk to you about?"

Looking to Matthew for support, Hattie said, "You had better sit down, Mama."

"Why?"

"Just trust us, Minerva," Matthew replied, as he took her hand and led her to a chair next to Dakota.

Sitting down, Minerva suddenly had a horrible feeling run through her body. "It's your Pa, isn't it?"

Choosing not to say anything, Hattie simply handed her mother the telegram Laville had given her earlier at the creek. Reading it, Minerva felt weak. She didn't know what to think. All her life, she had hoped that someday Newton would change his evil ways, but now with his death, she knew that he had died not having made any sort of recompense. That, more than anything, made her sad, as she knew that he would be held accountable for all the evil he had done."

"She be comin' around," Mary yelled, breaking the silence.

Without a second thought, everyone rushed to the settee where she lay. Even Minerva, who was still out of sorts, put her feelings aside and made her way to Laville's side.

Looking up groggily, Laville said, "Did I die?"

"No, you didn't be dying," Mary replied, "but you be givin' us quite a scare."

"How long was I out?"

"Quite some time, Lass. How you be feelin'?"

"My head hurts like the dickens, but other than that, I think I'm okay. How did I get here?"

"George found you unconscious in your buggy," Hattie responded kindly. "Apparently, after you finished talking with Matthew, Shannon, and I, you took off for town and passed out on the way. Luckily, George happened to be driving home from Gallatin, found you, and brought you home."

Suddenly remembering their conversation by the road, Laville's face went flush, and her demeanor was unusually soft. "Oh, Hattie, please forgive me for my terrible behavior earlier. I don't know what in the world came over me. I guess hearing of Pa's death was more of a shock than I realized. It wasn't until I was on my way back to town that it occurred to me that everything would be different from now on, because he won't be able to hurt any of us anymore."

Still not knowing of Newton's death, George, Mary, and Curtis were stunned. Even more stunned, though, was the family over

Laville's sudden compassion. Standing in disbelief, Shannon and Dakota could only shake their heads.

"But, Laville," Hattie answered cautiously, "you were so mean and unfeeling."

"I know, I know. I don't always handle things well, and I guess this was one of those times. I'm sorry, Hattie, please believe me."

Looking down into the eyes of what seemed like a total stranger, Hattie could see that Laville really was sincere and repentant for what she had said earlier. Glancing in Matthew's direction, Hattie looked for an explanation, but he could only shrug his shoulders, as her behavior had him stumped as well. It was not like Laville to be repentant for anything. Turning back toward her, Hattie didn't know what to think. "Are you sure you're feeling alright?"

"Yes," Laville replied, as she sat up on the settee. "Except for my head, I feel fine, and I'm sincerely sorry for what happened earlier." Reaching out, she took Hattie's hand. "Please forgive me."

Completely disarmed, Hattie replied, "All right, Laville, apology accepted." Turning her attention to her mother, Hattie took her hand and led her back to the fireplace. Speaking as tenderly as she could, she said, "Mama, we've got another problem. Before his death, Pa served Lorna with papers saying she and the children had to move out of their house in Keokuk."

"You're kidding."

"I'm afraid not. Shannon told me about it down by the creek today. I decided to do some things for her financially, but I really don't think that she should be alone during this time in her life."

"Oh, I agree with you one hundred percent, Hattie. What do you propose we do?"

"I thought that you could contact Lorna and invite her and the children to stay at Silver Creek with us, at least for a little while. She really needs a support system right now, and the children will love playing with each other. To me, it seems like a win-win situation."

Speaking up, Curtis said, "I don't understand, Hattie. If Pa's dead, why does Lorna have to move out her home?"

"The courts have already decided that she has no legal right to the property, Curtis. I know it is a rotten deal, but it is for the best. It will be better for Lorna to have a new start in life away from Keokuk, and with the money she is going to get from me, she'll be able to live anywhere she wants."

"Watch it, Lass," Mary interjected, shaking her head. "It be just like your Pa to still be a causin' pain and heartache, even from the grave."

* * *

Lorna and her children arrived within the week and were immediately accepted as part of the family. Lorna and Minerva struck up an instant friendship, and the kids loved the immensity and extravagance of the mansion. Their happiness took on a bitter taste, though, as Newton's body arrived a day later. Attached to the casket was a letter from the undertaker from Princeton.

Dear Morran Family,

I send my deepest condolences for your loss. I did all that I could to prepare the body, but I'm afraid that there is little left of it. He was very severely burnt from head to toe, making the identification very difficult. It's dealing with cases like this that make me wish I had taken on a different profession. Once again, please accept my condolences.

Sincerely,

Daniel Jenkins

After much deliberation by Hattie, Minerva, and Lorna, it was decided that, in spite of all the heartache he had caused, Newton's body should still be buried in the family cemetery at Silver Creek. For the sake of their children, both Minerva and Lorna remained poised and calm throughout the funeral.

The graveside service was kept short and simple. Both Lorna and Minerva sat at the head of Newton's grave, and each took a turn in speaking to their children. Reverend Walker had little to say about Newton, and not many people attended, as he had never been too well liked in Gallatin.

Finally, James, taking his place as patriarch of the family, stood before everyone and spoke in a commanding yet loving tone. "If there is one thing that you take from this service today, children, it is that no one man is the same to all people. Your father, Newton, was the perfect example of this. On the one hand, he lived, for the most part, a decent life in Keokuk with Lorna. More importantly, he also gave each of you the spark of life, which created your bodies. This marvelous process enabled your spirit to come to the earth, where you are to be tried and tested to see if you will be found worthy to return to our Heavenly Father. For this, all of you should be grateful to Newton. On the other hand, though, Newton performed many evil deeds and caused a great deal of pain to many. I don't think we need to go into them here today, because we all know what they are. The trick in life is to learn something from the deeds of those who have come and gone before us on this earth so that you may avoid similar pitfalls in your own life. Always remember, what you make of yourselves in this life is entirely up to you, as the only thing that limits you is yourself. You can do anything that you put your mind to, and don't allow yourself to get discouraged, for the impossible just takes a little bit longer."

Taking a deep breath, James continued, "All of you have blessed with loving mothers in Minerva and Lorna who have taught you right from wrong and good from evil. It is this stable foundation that will enable you to live happy and productive lives. What caused Newton to be the type of man he was, we may never know, but good can always be found, even in what appears to be the worst situation."

Looking first to Lorna's children, James stated kindly, "Because of your father's marriage to Minerva, you have the great blessings of older brothers and sisters to love you, care for you, and help guide you." Then, turning to Minerva's children, he said, "Those of you who are Minerva's children are certainly blessed that your father married Lorna, because now you have these little angels to be a part of your lives. These are definitely blessings, and if each of you will embrace life's blessings while living your lives as good men and women, you will survive every heartache and pitfall the adversary places in your paths. This I promise you in the name of the Lord Jesus Christ, Amen."

Never before had the family heard such hope and promise in such simple words, nor had they ever before felt the Holy Spirit as close to them as they did that day. Many even left Newton's grave holding each other's hands and resolving to make each day count for good.

As the family made their way back to the house, Hattie watched Laville very closely. The temporary compassion Laville showed after regaining consciousness only a few short days earlier was now only a fleeting memory, as she was back to her bitter, evil self. Pulling Shannon aside, she said, "For life of me of, Shannon, I can't understand Laville's violent mood swings. I really believed her the other day when she said she was sorry, but now, seeing that devious smile on her face during the service, I can't help but I think there is something seriously wrong with Laville."

"I could have told you that long ago," Shannon replied jokingly.

"No, I'm serious. There is something deeply wrong with her other than just her bad attitude. I don't know what it is, but it is almost as if she is a real life Dr. Jekyll and Mr. Hyde."

"You know what?" Shannon said, as if he had just remembered something. "You might be right. When I heard Laville talking the other night it reminded me of something, but I couldn't put my finger on it until just now."

"What?"

"Do you remember when Abner threw you down the stairs a couple years back?"

"How could I forget? I almost died."

"Well, while you were unconscious, Laville acted very strangely. Just like the other day, she was completely sincere and compassionate, totally unlike how she usually is. At the time, I just brushed it off, but now that it's happened again, it makes me wonder."

"I know what you mean," Hattie replied solemnly. "Laville is truly a mystery. We may never really understand her 'secrets of the heart', but as God as my witness, I will never give up trying to reach her."

Amazed at Hattie's love and devotion, Shannon said, "Sis, you're an angel."

"Not hardly," she replied. "I just do what I think the Savior would do."

Entering the house and making their way to the parlor, Hattie and Shannon found Laville ready to toast their father's death. She had glasses poured with champagne for everyone. Raising her glass, she said, "To freedom. Newton, may you rot in hell." Hearing Laville's callous words, shock and disgust fell upon the family members. Hattie stood quietly by, saying nothing, knowing that it was her mother's place to speak to Laville.

"For Heaven's sake, Laville, put that glass down right now," Minerva said, as she grabbed Laville's arm and lowered it. "Your conduct is inexcusable. I'll not let you embarrass me in front of Lorna and these young children by toasting Newton's death."

Laville's eyes filled with tears, as she slammed her glass down on the end table near her. "But, Mama, I hated him so much; you know I did."

"Yes, Dear, we know that. He was mean to all of us. Yet, no matter how bad he treated us, he was an entirely different man with Lorna and her children. He was the person to them that I hoped he would be for us. I know that that doesn't excuse his despicable behavior, but it is morally wrong for us to rejoice in his, or anyone's, death."

Sensing the rage and turmoil that Laville was suffering, Matthew ran to her side and with great compassion opened his arms to embrace her. Collapsing into his strong grasp, Laville sobbed uncontrollably for several minutes. Then, just as abruptly as she collapsed, she bolted out of his arms, ran out of the house, climbed into her buggy, and sped away.

That night as Hattie reflected on everything that had happened, she worried about Laville's increasingly volatile behavior. Finding no answers to explain the reason for Laville's deep-rooted hatred, Hattie tried to get some sleep, but it was to no avail, as she kept having the most horrible dreams. At first the dreams centered only on

Laville and her behavior after the funeral, but as Hattie tossed and turned the night away, the dreams became more and more disturbing. In one dream she saw Mary screaming through the darkness at some- one, but at whom, she didn't know. In another, Hattie saw a huge explosion that shook her clear to her soul and left her awake in a cold sweat. Then, after she finally got to sleep again, she dreamt the unthinkable. She dreamt that she saw her Pa, alive. Sitting straight up in bed, the image of his face gave Hattie the chills.

Getting up and walking to the window, she dismissed his appear- ance in her mind to the funeral, and sleepily, she gazed out at the sun starting to break through the blackness of the night. The sunrise used to have such a calming influence on Hattie's soul, but now with time running short before the Judge's deadline, all it meant was that she was one day closer to Ira's imminent death.